HUGH WALTERS

FIRST

ON THE MOON

TEMPO BOOKS

GROSSET & DUNLAP

NEW YORK

FIRST ON THE MOON

Since time began there was no contest more fantastic than this one—the rocket *Columbus* and the rocket *Lenin* hurtling toward the moon, each carrying a human passenger intent on making the first landing on its surface.

Representing the Western powers is Chris Godfrey, the first man to be launched into space. On the other side of the world, at a secret site, Serge Smyslov has passed the most rigorous tests and is confident that he will be the first human to set foot on earth's satellite and claim it as a Soviet possession. Almost to the second the two young men blast off and are borne moonward, following an identical flight path. So begins the suspenseful race for the moon, with the whole world, both East and West, watching and listening as the two pioneers pursue their parallel routes farther and farther into untracked space.

Excitement mounts when Chris and Serge land near each other in the crater of Plato and set out to explore the lunar landscape, Chris in his elaborate space suit, Serge in his mobile minitank. The ideological conflict between their two worlds explodes into violent action when the two finally meet, only to be equally threatened by mysterious cloud waves that sweep across the moon's surface, paralyzing their power to act. Their only chance to return safely to earth, they both realize, lies in mutual cooperation, but will the politicians of the East and West agree to this? Chris, Serge and the world wait tensely for the decision as the deadly clouds draw nearer, and the chances for a successful return flight become more and more remote.

All the excitement and drama of man's conquest of space are here blended into a timely, action-packed thriller, backed by a wealth of scientific detail.

This TEMPO BOOKS *edition contains the complete text of the original hard-cover edition, published by Criterion Books, Inc. at $3.50*

TEMPO BOOKS

FIRST ON THE MOON

CHAPTER 1

"A landing must be made on the moon."

So concluded the secret report prepared by a joint committee of the foremost scientists of Britain, France, the United States, and West Germany, and presented to their respective governments.

Mr. Beaumont, the British prime minister, carefully placed on his desk the neatly typewritten pages he had just read, and leaned back in his chair. His mind went back to that terrible period, just over a year ago, when the whole world had been menaced by deadly radiation coming from mysterious artificial structures that had appeared on the moon's surface.

He recalled the sudden closing of atomic power stations all over the earth and the frightening effects the radiation was beginning to have on men, women, and children. Only by the pooling of the best brains in the world, by the concentrated effort of the greatest scientists and technicians—and by the dauntless courage of one young man—had the people of Earth been saved from a fate that had seemed certain.

The Premier recalled those ghastly days when world-wide panic was barely held in check, while out in

Australia men sweated round the clock to prepare the giant rockets that carried the atomic warheads. It had been necessary for a Levy beacon—apparatus for guiding the missiles to their objective—to be placed on the moon as close as possible to the malignant domes. Only a human being launched into an orbit round the moon could place the beacon in position, and Chris Godfrey had done the job magnificently.

Well, the atomic rockets had done what they were meant to do. They had landed accurately on the source of radiation, and, in the greatest man-made explosion that had ever taken place, had blasted the alien domes to fragments. The radiation had ceased and never reoccurred. Yet the governments of the world were worried; worried about who—or what—had constructed the domes and the strange cone with them. They feared that whoever was responsible would try again, perhaps next time from some invulnerable place.

It was vital that more should be known about conditions around the area where the domes were destroyed; whether the destruction was total, or if there were any evidences of new activity around Pico—that sharp little mountain peak that stood out from the lunar plain. If possible, something should be learned, too, about the builders of the domes. So an international committee of scientists had been formed to study the situation and to advise on a course of action. It was the report of this committee that Mr. Beaumont had been studying.

In response to a bell, a private secretary entered the room.

"I'd like you to summon the Cabinet for three o'clock," the Prime Minister said.

As the official withdrew, Mr. Beaumont picked up the report again and turned over its pages. Yet his mind was not so much on the typewritten words before him as on the astonishing refusal of Soviet Russia to take part in the work of the committee. Following the international rivalry that had culminated in the struggle to launch bigger and better artificial satellites, the world had been frightened by the radiation menace into acting in unison. Rivalries had been forgotten, differences overcome, and it seemed that the era of co-operation had dawned at last.

It was the wholehearted working together by American, Russian, and Commonwealth scientists which had made the destruction of the domes of Pico possible. What great progress was possible if this friendly co-operation could be maintained! Yet within a few weeks of the removal of that universal threat East and West had begun to drift apart, just as they had done after the Second World War.

The curt Soviet refusal to join the international scientific committee still rankled with the statesmen of Britain and the United States. France and Germany, the two western countries most advanced technically, had been invited to take the Soviet's place.

What was the U.S.S.R. proposing to do about the lunar domes? Surely Russia must be as much concerned about them as the rest of the world was, for Russian industry and the Russian people also had suffered from their baleful effects. Perhaps the Soviet Union was proposing to make investigations on its own. But why? What lay behind this new attitude? Mr. Beaumont searched without success for an answer to this latest Russian enigma.

Promptly at three o'clock that afternoon Her Majesty's Ministers met in the Cabinet room to consider the scientists' report. In each of the other participating countries governments were giving equally anxious thought to what their experts had said, for it was agreed that within the next forty-eight hours all must decide whether or not to follow the recommendations of the report. Little wonder, then, that the discussions were long and searching. In the end the governments all came to the same conclusion: that a close investigation of the moon and the domes was essential.

Once this vital decision had been made, the four countries agreed unanimously to throw into the project the whole of their resources, and to lose no time in carrying it out. The men who had drawn up the report were authorized to implement this undertaking as quickly as possible. It was to become known as Operation Columbus, in tribute to a great adventurer of the past.

It was a momentous occasion when Dr. Elton Rosenberg, the internationally famous American rocket expert who had acted as chairman of the scientific committee, announced to it that all the governments concerned had requested it to become an executive body, with unlimited power to translate its report into action. As the full significance of his words sank in, Dr. Rosenberg looked around at the score of men gathered in that rather dingy room in a huge building in Horseferry Road, London.

Here were some of the world's most brilliant men. A few of them had been his friends and colleagues for many years; others he had never met until they joined his committee. There were four fellow Americans, including the director of the Mount Palomar Observatory, which housed the world's largest telescope, the famous two hundred inch one. The British contingent included the Astronomer Royal, Dr. Raymond Clarke, and Sir Leo Frayling. Professor Marcel Berger, a famous physicist, represented France; and Dr. Heinrich Zimmerman, a brilliant chemist, was the member from Germany.

The first task before the Columbus Committee was to appoint a leader. He would need to be almost a superman to hold together and coordinate the work of this brilliant group. More than one of those present thought of Sir George Benson, perhaps the world's foremost rocket expert. But Sir George was not available, for he was still terribly crippled by the appalling injuries he had received more than a year ago in the most fantastic rescue operation the world had ever known.

Another man under consideration was a member of the committee, Sir Leo Frayling. It was he who had directed that memorable effort which had destroyed the domes. But Sir Leo had driven his fellow workers on with a singleminded ruthlessness that had made the others almost hate him. It was feared that in spite of his brilliant mind his utter lack of humanity would make it impossible to get some of the best men in the field to work on the project. It was Sir George who had held things together before. If only he were able to do so again, by being an active worker on the project, Sir Leo might once more be a desirable director.

Some miles away, in a white Georgian house on the outskirts of Cambridge, Sir George was entertaining Chris. With the aid of his sticks he hobbled painfully from the dining room to his library. Chris was tempted to offer assistance, but he knew this would be tactless. Instead, he followed slowly behind his friend until Sir George settled himself awkwardly in a fireside chair.

Every evidence of Sir George's disabilities brought back to Chris the painful memory of that fantastic trip into outer space—and back. Sir Leo Frayling, in complete charge of the international effort to destroy the source of lunar radiation, had pursued his objective with such ruthless disregard for any personal considerations that he had sent Chris on a rocket journey from which he knew there could be no return. It had been Frayling's decision that the life of one person could not stand in the way of salvation for millions. Then Benson, aware for the first time of Frayling's plan, had revealed himself as a man of unimaginable courage. He had rescued Chris in the face of almost certain disaster, and had nearly paid for it with his life.

Throughout that painful year Sir George had fought

grimly to regain his health. After several months in hospitals he had been allowed to go home, but he was told that he would never walk again. Yet his indomitable will had proved the doctors wrong. Now his steps, though painful and slow, were aided only by a pair of canes.

Chris had watched his friend's struggle with sympathy and growing hope. If his body had been mangled and torn, his mind was as clear and incisive as ever. Indeed, Sir George's long-enforced physical inactivity had given him the opportunity for much study and thought. He had been retained as nominal director of the Australian Rocket Research Establishment, but really it was his deputy director, Mr. W. H. R. G. Gillanders, who was carrying on the work there.

Sir George had been greatly disappointed not to be a member of the international scientific committee; it was his greatest ambition to serve with his old colleagues once more. Chris, perhaps more than anyone else, knew how he longed to return to active life. Before he left his friend's house that night Chris had made up his mind to try to help him do so.

Next morning, Saturday, Chris took an early train to London. He was going to visit no other than Sir Leo Frayling. After the amazing rescue, Sir Leo had gone out of his way to give Sir George all credit and unstinted praise for it. He had visited both him and Chris in the Woomera hospital and had appeared more human than they had ever known him to be. During the past year Chris had seen Sir Leo several times, and while their relationship was not exactly warm, it was not unfriendly.

As Chris had planned, he bumped into Sir Leo, seemingly by accident, as he entered a coffee bar near his office. Sir Leo seemed delighted, and insisted on taking Chris in with him. As they waited for the coffee to cool, Chris chatted away about his college work.

Then, after the first sip, he plunged into the real object of his visit.

"Sir Leo," he began, "I spent yesterday evening with Uncle George. He sends his regards to you."

"Good. How is he? I'll have to go along and see him as soon as I can."

"He's better, much better. Of course, it's his will-power that's pulling him through, but I don't think he'll get much farther without help."

"What do you mean?" Frayling asked.

"He's eating his heart out to get back to work again," Chris said, "I'm sure it would go a long way to help his recovery if he had something positive to do. I wondered if you might help him."

"It's funny you should say that," Sir Leo said thoughtfully. "We were talking about him only yesterday afternoon on that international committee. We need him with us. In fact, he would be just the man to direct the job, if he were physically fit."

"But he's as keen as mustard," Chris said eagerly. "His mind's more active than ever. I don't know about his directing the committee, but surely he could be a part of it."

"No, Chris. This committee had been given a vital job to do." Frayling spoke so quietly that his voice could only just be heard against the noise of the juke-box in the corner. "I expect you can guess what we've been working on. Well, we've been given the green light to carry out a job as vital as and perhaps more difficult than the long-range destruction of the domes. Operation Columbus, it's been christened. You can put two and two together and get a pretty good idea of what we've got to do. Benson isn't thought to be fit enough to take any part at all, let alone run the show, as we'd all like him to do."

"Then who's going to be director?"

"Haven't the foggiest idea. Rosenberg's been chairman while we were a study group, but he flatly refuses to take charge now we've cleared the decks for action."

"What about you, Sir Leo?"

"Once was enough for me, Chris."

"I wonder," Chris said, half aloud. Then he added, "But will you go and talk to Sir George? You said that you owe him a visit. You'll be able to see for yourself whether or not he's capable of helping you," Chris persisted.

"Yes, I'll certainly go sometime, but I can't manage it just now," Sir Leo sighed. "I'm appallingly busy."

"Sir Leo, do please go and see him soon. I'd like you to have a talk with him."

"Very well," Frayling agreed, with surprising affability. "I'll go down tomorrow afternoon. Will that satisfy you?"

"Yes, thanks! It'll cheer up Uncle George no end to talk shop with you. Thanks a lot. Now I'll run along and let you get on with whatever mysterious task you're engaged on." Chris smiled.

They drank their coffee, paid the bill, stepped outside, and paused on the pavement.

"Thank you again, Sir Leo," Chris said.

Frayling smiled. "Glad to oblige," he said.

They shook hands firmly, and went their separate ways.

CHAPTER 2

As the train rattled him back to Cambridge, Chris thought of the talk he'd had with Sir Leo. This Operation Columbus must be connected with further investigation of those domes. Even though they'd been destroyed, the explanation for them was still to be found. "As vital as and perhaps more difficult than the long-range destruction," Sir Leo had said. Surely that could only mean a much closer inspection. Suddenly Chris's heart almost stood still at the thought that sprang into his mind. *Was Operation Columbus to be a landing on the moon?*

He sat bolt upright with the shock of the idea. A landing? The first human to step onto another world! Columbus? That was it! It all tied up. So the committee was going to organize the first crossing of space, and—if all went well—someone would set foot on Earth's companion! What an achievement that would be! What a step toward man's conquest of space!

For some reason—perhaps for a number of reasons—a certain ambition began to grow in Chris's mind. Once it had started, it grew and grew, until by the time he reached Cambridge one thought alone possessed him. He wanted to be the person to land on the moon!

It was not the ordinary romantic ambition so many young people have when they become interested in space travel. Neither was it a desire to make a heroic sacrifice for science and humanity. It certainly was no longing for notoriety. Chris had already had more than his share of that and had hated it. Perhaps it was because, having been the first human being to be launched in a rocket and then, two years later, the first to make an orbit around the moon, he wanted to complete the job by making an actual landing. Anyway, he knew that, whatever the risk, he wanted to be the one selected for the undertaking.

As he stepped from the train Chris's thoughts went back to his two previous adventures. On the first occasion Sir George Benson, whom he'd only just met, had asked him to go. He could remember the shock he'd had when the scientist had put the suggestion to him, and how he had eventually agreed to be launched in a rocket. His experiences on that trip still made him shudder. They were still very real to him when Sir George—this time at the request of the government—had asked him to undertake an even more ambitious voyage.

Chris remembered how upset he had been to think that, having almost lost his life on the first venture, he should be asked to go on a second, beside which the first appeared almost child's play. He had gone, of course, when he learned what it meant to his fellow men. He was glad now that he had been able to overcome his fears and undertake that ghastly mission. Now, for the first time, he himself wanted to go, and he determined that nothing should stop him.

For the second evening running he called on Sir George Benson.

"I saw Sir Leo this morning," he said. "Managed to catch him just as he was going into the coffee bar next to his office. He's been very busy lately on that committee of his. It seems that he's going to be even more tied up in the future, because there's something pretty big looming up. You know, Uncle George, my bet is that they're going to attempt a landing on the moon."

"That wouldn't surprise me," Sir George answered. "It's the logical outcome of present research. I gather there's been an amazing development in rocket fuels during the last few months—they're getting some pretty high exhaust velocities from the exotic boron compounds. A landing and a safe return should be perfectly feasible."

"My bet is that Operation Columbus—that's what they call it—is designed to find out more about those domes. No one has a theory about their origin, have they, sir?"

"I wouldn't say that. Many people, I expect, have their own ideas. I must confess that during my enforced inactivity during the last few months I've given the matter a great deal of thought myself. But I don't suppose anyone would be interested in *my* theories any longer."

"Don't you believe it, Uncle George. As a matter of fact Sir Leo told me he's coming over tomorrow to have a talk with you. I would tell him your theories, if I were you," Chris said eagerly.

"Frayling's coming here tomorrow? I shall be glad to see him," Sir George exclaimed. "Yes, of course I'll tell him my ideas about the domes. At least, if he'll listen to me."

"Perhaps you'll get an invitation to work on the Columbus Committee after all."

"That's hardly likely," Benson said, "though I must confess that I'd go to almost any lengths to join it."

"You know, Uncle George, someone has to make this landing. I wonder if I could go," Chris said, almost timidly.

Benson looked at him in amazement. "You go?

Haven't you had enough already? You don't seriously mean you'd like to be launched in a rocket again?"

"Indeed I should. I'd like to land on the moon just as much as you'd like to work on the Columbus Committee," Chris replied.

"I don't suppose there's any more chance of one happening than the other," Benson said, "so we may both just as well forget about the whole thing."

"I'm not so sure," Chris persisted. "After he's seen you, Sir Leo may be able to persuade the committee to take you on. As for me—well, I've had previous experience," he ended with a smile.

"You certainly have, Christopher. Ah well, we shall see."

"Look, Uncle George. Let's make a pact. If you get roped in on Operation Columbus, will you try to get me that rocket trip?"

"You're an optimistic young man, aren't you? If it will please you, I'll agree." Benson laughed, but Chris insisted on shaking hands on their bargain.

True to his promise, Sir Leo Frayling called to see Sir George Benson on Sunday afternoon. Sir George greeted him cordially. Not so long ago these two had been bitter enemies, but all that was now past, wiped out by those tremendous events in the Australian desert. The two men were soon so deeply immersed in scientific conversation that they were both surprised when Sir George's housekeeper came in with tea.

Frayling had only intended this to be a short courtesy call made to satisfy Christopher, but as hour after hour slipped by unnoticed, he felt a growing conviction that Benson should—indeed must—work on the Columbus Committee. In spite of his physical handicap, the crystal clarity of his intellect would be a tremendous asset. Besides, there was Sir George's startling yet convincing theory about the origin of the domes.

When he met his colleagues on Monday afternoon, Frayling surprised them all by the account he gave of his visit the previous day. After a certain amount of hesitation, the committee agreed to invite Benson to appear before it the following day. Sir Leo himself telephoned the invitation and promised to pick Sir George up in his car.

That Tuesday meeting was memorable. No one present would forget the impact made on them by the crippled scientist. He spoke forcefully, though quietly, and so impressed them all with the vigor of his mind that there was spontaneous applause when he had finished speaking. With a suggestion of embarrassment, he bowed stiffly and hobbled from the room, followed by Sir Leo.

On Friday morning Frayling, Rosenberg, Berger, and Zimmerman visited Cambridge to invite Sir George Benson to become a member of the Columbus Committee. Whatever his feelings were, Benson concealed them, and only a slight flush betrayed his emotion. With composure, he thanked the deputation and agreed to accept the appointment. He would move up to a London flat, taking his housekeeper with him. Transportation would be provided by the government, so that his physical handicap would not interfere with his work on the committee.

That same day it was decided to offer the Committee directorship to Frayling. The other members of the committee had decided individually and in informal tete-a-tetes that Sir Leo's coldness and capacity for arousing antagonism in his associates was more than offset by his scientific brilliance and by his successful experience in the previous space project. After some hesitation Frayling accepted the post. His duties would begin at once, it was agreed, so that Operation Columbus could swing into action without delay.

As the door closed behind the committee delegation, a sudden horrible thought struck Sir George. It was his promise to Christopher to try to have him chosen for the lunar landing if he himself joined the committee!

He had made the promise lightly, never dreaming that he would have anything to do with the project. Now here he was, actually on the committee. How, then, did he stand about his promise to young Godfrey? He must think this thing through carefully.

As soon as Chris came face to face with Benson, two days later, he knew that something had happened. Before the scientist had time to tell him that he had been invited to be on the Columbus Committee, Chris sensed the news. He sensed, too, that this subtle change in Sir George was an indication something was worrying him. Chris wondered what it was. He did not stay long, for he could see that Benson's mind was already busy planning the task ahead. Nor did either of them mention the pact between them.

Right from its start on Monday morning, the Columbus Committee was controlled with icy efficiency by its new chairman. Benson and Rosenberg, who had known him in the past, realized—as the others would soon—that to work under Sir Leo was an unsettling experience. No one else seemed to have such capacity for causing resentment among his colleagues, yet no one commanded greater respect. Under Frayling's direction no personal considerations existed. The success of Operation Columbus became the only thing that mattered. Sir Leo was, as Benson and Rosenberg knew, capable of a ruthless pursuit of his objective. They knew, too, that if any man could drive Operation Columbus to success, it was he.

Outline plans for Operation Columbus were rapidly sketched in. Decisions were made about fuels, specification of the rocket vehicle, the instruments to be carried, launching site, and the best possible date, direction, and velocity for the actual flight. Details were worked out for the lunar landing maneuver, the program of exploration, the take-off back to Earth, and the method of re-entry into the atmosphere with an ultimate landing close to the place from which the rocket had been fired.

All these and countless other items were discussed minutely, but one subject—perhaps the most important of all—was never mentioned. Who was to be the human being to be launched across space? Whose was to be the responsibility for finding out more about the domes? Who, in fact, would be the first person to set foot on the moon?

CHAPTER 3

"The choice is yours, Boronoff," the commissar was saying. "You will take charge of our undertaking or you can use your talents in the New Regions."

In spite of himself, the Russian scientist shuddered slightly. The New Regions which the commissar had mentioned were the vast territories that the Soviet Union was feverishly developing from the wild and empty lands near the Arctic Circle. Here, in a rigorous climate, thousands of people were toiling to build new steelworks, rolling mills, coal mines, factories. Some of the workers went there voluntarily, persuaded in a fervor of patriotism by the most able propaganda machine in the world.

Others were sent there for various reasons, usually because they had deviated from the Communist party line, or because they were beginning to have ideas and thoughts of their own. In the days of the Tsars inconvenient people were sent to Siberia. Today they were "promoted" to a job in the New Regions. Professor Boronoff knew that few returned.

"I will do as you wish," he said, and hated himself for saying it.

Boronoff was Russia's top rocket expert. He was, too, the physicist who had been largely responsible for the design and manufacture of atomic warheads for use in intercontinental ballistic missiles. It was he who had been designated to work with the Anglo-American team in the tremendous joint undertaking that had destroyed the domes of Pico. During the months he had known his Western colleagues, Boronoff had conceived a great respect—even an affection—for them. Like most men of science, he deplored the artificial barriers to universal co-operation that politicians had imposed.

When these barriers had been lowered for the International Geophysical Year program, then again for the destruction of the domes, Boronoff hoped and believed that a new age of brotherhood had dawned between the scientists and technicians of the world. He had been bitterly disappointed to find that the rulers in the Kremlin had other ideas. With sadness he gave up all idea of working with his British and American friends again.

Indeed, he was now being requested to operate in opposition to them. The commissar had explained to him very clearly that the Supreme Soviet had decided to pursue its own line in further ventures into space. Conscious of Western concern about the origins of the lunar domes, Russia had decided to investigate independently—and at the same time to stake a claim to possession of Earth's satellite. Nonco-operation with the West, therefore, was the new order of the day. The Soviet Union must—and should—put the first human being on the moon.

Boronoff thought long about the bitter experience of many former colleagues—countrymen who had dared to question Communist wisdom. However eminent a scientist might be, he had to fit his thoughts, his actions, even his discoveries and theories, to the pattern required by the Communist State. Little wonder, then, that he had appreciated his opportunity to work with

Western scientists, unhampered by politicians. Now he was back amid the old political restrictions, free to work only on the line laid down—which was at all costs to beat the West in the race to the moon.

That Russia could beat the rest of the world, Boronoff had no doubt, for she could draw on the immense army of highly trained scientists and technicians that was pouring in an ever-increasing flood from the new universities and schools. She could pursue an objective with an unswerving purpose which no Western state could hope to match.

Here there was no concern for the effects on the national economy of any undertaking, however gigantic. Here the ruling party was not hindered by the hesitations and doubts of an opposition. Now that the Communist aim had crystallized into a conquest of the moon, the whole mighty machinery of the nation would be geared to ensure the success of the project. Boronoff asked the commissar for his instructions.

The great Soviet rocket center on the coast of the Black Sea was very different from the busy little establishment at Woomera. The Russian experimental area seemed like a vast open prison. All inhabitants for many miles around had been removed and all persons entering or leaving were subject to the strictest possible security check. Even top scientists were constantly stopped and made to produce documents of identity. All personnel engaged in the area were compelled to attend regular political lectures, and Party commissars were in evidence everywhere.

On the other hand, the rocket workers had plenty of equipment. Nothing that a powerful state could provide was lacking. All material requirements were quickly supplied. When a technical problem arose, a whole army of highly trained men and women would attack it and produce a solution in the shortest possible time. There was no question of cost or conservation of materials. Only the result mattered; only the objective was important. And that objective was—to reach the moon before the West did!

The plane that touched down at one of the airfields in the Rocket Area was a T.U. 109—the latest Soviet jet plane, used only by important Party officials. This day its passengers were a score of scientists collected from all parts of the Soviet Union. These were the men who were to lead the great Russian effort. Professor Boronoff led his colleagues from the plane to greet the waiting officials. He was not a happy man.

Barely thirty minutes later another aircraft landed at the same field. Again it was a T.U. 109, but this time it was a dozen young men who emerged from it. The officials who met them looked curiously at these passengers. Some of them appeared to be barely seventeen, and none seemed more than twenty-five. They were a strange contrast to the party of middle-aged scientists who had preceded them. What were these young men, who seemed more suitable for a football field, doing in the rocket area? Only the officials who took charge of them knew the answer—that one of these young men would eventually step onto the moon.

Like the scientists, the twelve young men came from different parts of the Soviet Union. They had been selected months before for their fitness and intelligence, and had been undergoing strenuous training and conditioning for the task that lay ahead. Each of them had been subjected to all sorts of tests to make sure he would be capable of what was required. Now they had arrived in the rocket area for final training and for the ultimate selection of the one to be launched across space.

Within a few days of his arrival, Boronoff had things running to his liking. The huge, three-stage rocket was rapidly taking shape. More than a score of brilliant mathematicians were working out the best possible trajectory for the lunar rocket, and then for its return back to Earth. A team of astronomers was studying the lunar surface by means of powerful telescopes and by photography from lunar rockets in orbit around the moon.

Results had reached Earth by television and by two cameras that had been safely brought back. These photographs, obtained by rocket and satellite, had the great advantage of clarity. They showed far greater detail than any obtained from Earth, even with the best telescope, for the exposures made in empty space had none of the limits caused by the dense atmosphere and clouds of dust which blanket Earth. After studying all the information available, the astronomers unanimously recommended that the landing area should be within the dark crater called Plato.

Another problem which the engineers and technicians faced was: how should the first man on the moon make his exploration? For years Soviet scientists had favored the idea that the lunar rocket should carry a small tracked vehicle like a miniature tank. The caterpillar tracks would enable it to travel across the rough surface, and the vehicle itself would protect the explorer from the hazards of extreme temperatures, lack of atmosphere, and possible impact of meteors.

Design and manufacture of this minitank was a difficult problem. It must permit its passenger to drive about for several days, carrying motive power, oxygen, food, and insulation. At the same time, weight must be kept to an absolute minimum because of the terrific cost in rocket fuel of every pound of weight landed on the moon.

Each of the twelve young men from whom the lunar explorer would be selected was desperately anxious to be chosen. For many months it had been constantly repeated to them that their whole lives were now designed with one object in view—to undertake this work for the greater glory of the Soviet Union. Every day they ate, breathed, and slept with no other thought.

[27]

Their routine was carefully calculated to fit them for the task. Just as, some years before, a number of dogs had been trained for launching in the Sputniks, so these young people were conditioned with scientific thoroughness. Psychologists and doctors were constantly devising new ordeals for them. Each had actually been launched in a rocket to a great height, and had returned safely to Earth. It was going to be a difficult job to make the final selection, so readily had they all responded to their training.

Yet, unknown to his fellows and to the scientists in whose constant care they were, one of these young men was an exception. His name was Serge Smyslov. Twenty-two years old, slim, wiry, athletic, Serge was a product of the great University of Leningrad. He had short curly black hair, wide dark eyes, and an olive skin. He had been studying to become a physicist, and had done so well that his professors predicted a brilliant future for him.

Like the eleven other young men, Serge had undergone successfully all the rigorous training and tests, all the psychological conditioning, all the detailed instruction. To his mentor and to his companions he seemed admirably fitted to the task for which he might be selected. But the psychologists had failed to uncover something locked deeply in Serge's heart. Serge was afraid—or, rather, he was afraid of fear.

How he had managed to conceal this, he never knew. Perhaps if he had been just plain scared it would have been discovered easily, but to be afraid of showing fear was a much more complex emotion. So rare were his moments of privacy that the young Russian had little opportunity of giving way to this private feeling, which perhaps was why it was concealed so deeply. Consciously he was as anxious to be selected as the others, but subconsciously there was within him a great dread.

Under Boronoff's direction the preparations went on

apace. The engineers had straightened out all the problems connected with the minitank. One was nearing completion and a second one—the one to be used on the moon—was well under way. As soon as Number 1 was ready it would be tested exhaustively on territory similar to what was expected to be encountered in the lunar landing area. These tests would show if any modifications were necessary in Number 2, and would also give an opportunity of training whoever was selected for the trip. The final choice, therefore, could not be long delayed. On Boronoff's instructions the psychologists and physiologists must make their decision soon.

The professor's order was received by the dozen candidates with relief, but the men who had to make the decision were anything but happy. For weeks they had been trying to eliminate all but one of their proteges, yet all the young men had come through every trial the scientists could devise, and the final selection was no nearer. Physically and mentally there was nothing to choose between them. They were all a hundred per cent fit; they were all alert, quick-witted, and of high mental ability. How could the choice be made? It was one of the psychologists who at last suggested a ruthless method of deciding.

Briefly, he proposed the construction of a dozen containers approximately the size of the interior of the minitank. Whoever was chosen would be sealed in this little vehicle before the rocket left Earth, would remain in it during the voyage to the moon and for the period on the lunar surface, and would return in it to the rocket for the journey back to Earth. Only when the rocket had landed safely would the minitank be removed and its occupant released.

The scientist's idea was to shut the twelve young men up in the containers and to simulate as nearly as possible the conditions of the voyage. Oxygen, food and water would be sealed in with them, and they would be shut off from all except radio contact with the outside world. The young man who could endure these conditions for the longest period would be chosen.

Boronoff had no choice but to agree to the psychologist's proposal. Work on the containers was put in hand. The victims received the news stolidly. Eleven of them, perhaps, were not unduly worried, but Serge felt inside him that peculiar little quake which he would not admit was fear.

Within a week the twelve containers were ready. They were placed alongside each other in a long low building. Inside each were put the necessities of life for a month. In each also was a button which the occupant could press when he could no longer tolerate the confinement; he would then be released immediately. Continuous watch would be maintained, but the radio was to be used only in an emergency. None of the occupants of the containers would know how his competitors were faring, and none would have any way of keeping track of the passage of time.

Promptly at noon on the day chosen, the twelve young men stood outside their temporary prisons. A small crowd of scientists gathered around to witness the start of their ordeal. Boronoff, who disliked the whole proceeding intensely, had perforce to be there. He observed that each of the dozen young men seemed outwardly calm. Giving the signal for the test to begin, he watched the young Russians step inside their containers. At once the doors were tightly sealed and the time of waiting began.

Inside, each young man took stock of his confined quarters. He saw a light shining, and heard a gentle hiss coming from the oxygen supply. The red alarm button stood out prominently, reminding him that it had only to be pressed for the ordeal to be ended. But each young man determined to be the last to be released, for each one wished above all else to qualify for man's greatest adventure.

[30]

Like the other, Serge soon began to get bored by the inactivity. For the hundredth time he looked over all the things in the small cabin, and always his eyes came back to the red release button. How were the others getting on? he wondered. Were they too finding this confinement tedious? How long had he been inside? One hour, three hours, four? Anyway, it was too early to start worrying about how long he'd been in. Better relax and let time look after itself.

Ah! He'd try some of the food pellets and sip some of the drinking fluid that were in tubes clipped to the side of the compartment. Slowly he chewed the almost tasteless pellet, which was about the size of a table-tennis ball. In this was concentrated as much food as there would be in a good-sized meal. Many times in the past he and his companions had had to subsist for weeks at a time on this space diet. It was adequate but uninteresting. Just a sip of the cool liquid was sufficient to allay thirst.

Serge completed his meal—if it could be called a meal—and then sat back in the seat. He closed his eyes. Perhaps he could sleep to pass some of the time away. How long he sat with his eyes closed, Serge did not know. Suddenly he started up. He must have dozed off—or had he slept for a long time? Automatically he lifted his wrist to look at his watch, then remembered that all watches had been taken away. He could have slept for a few minutes or a few hours.

In the building where the twelve containers stood in a neat row, a score of men interested in the test were watching. Regularly throughout day and night the watchers were relieved by others who took their places. Not a sound came from the cabin-like structures to indicate whether their occupants were alive or dead.

If only he knew what time or what day it was! Serge had never before realized how important was the observation of time. How long had he been inside? And how were the others faring? He felt an almost overpowering need to know the answer. Relentlessly, the cabin light shone and the oxygen valve hissed. Periodically, when he felt hunger or thirst, he would eat and drink, but there was no way of judging what the intervals were. Every so often his eyes would wander toward the alarm button. Perspiration stood on his forehead as he forced from his mind the desire to end this ordeal by pressing it. He beat his forehead with clenched fists in his effort to maintain self-control.

"I must stick it out, I must," he said. Then he realized that he had spoken aloud—as indeed he had been doing for some time. Every thought that came into his head he'd unconsciously expressed in words. This will never do, he told himself, and he pursed his lips grimly. Yet within a comparatively short time he caught himself speaking aloud again. Vainly he tried to sleep, but it seemed that the enforced inactivity of his body was somehow being compensated for by the increased activity of his brain. Sleep would not come; or if it did, it came only in fitful snatches.

Now the confinement was becoming almost unendurable. He must press that button, for he could go on no longer. No, no! He dare not. If he did, perhaps he would be the first to give in. The horror of this possibility shook him, and for a time he was no longer tempted to make the fateful move. Then the sense of imprisonment descended on him again with redoubled force. He stretched out his hand to within an inch of the button, but with a cry of agony he forced himself to desist.

Calm now! Be calm! Serge fought heroically to master his feelings. He even forced himself to sing, and to pass the hours away he sang every song that he could remember. He kept this up until he drove himself almost crazy. Then he tried relaxing and breathing as slowly as he could, counting his respirations. If he breathed five or six times a minute, that was something over three hundred an hour. A thousand would probably mean the passing of three hours. How high could he count? He wasn't much past the first thousand when he found he kept forgetting what number he had reached. Finally, in a burst of anger, he gave up.

Occasionally he slept, and at times he ate and drank. Now all his conscious thoughts were engaged in a titanic struggle to keep his finger off the fateful button. Time after time he dragged his arm back to his side. No, it would never do to give up. How they would all laugh and jeer at him! How terrible it would be if he were one of the early ones to be released— perhaps even the first.

One-two-three. Four. Now he was counting the seconds as they slid past. He must fight—fight for time to pass. Five hundred and sixty-nine. Five hundred and seventy. His head was reeling. He couldn't go on any longer. He must! No, he couldn't. With horror, almost as if it belonged to another person, Serge watched his arm rise from his side and his finger press hard on the button.

The young Russian shrank back onto his seat, horrified at what he'd done. It hadn't seemed like himself at all. Something had come over him and he'd seen his hand ring the alarm as if it had a will of its own. Already he could hear sounds of the door being unfastened. The shame of it! He'd never be able to look anyone in the face again. Trembling, he covered his face with his hands and waited for the worst. Every second he expected to hear a sarcastic torrent of words as his instructors faced him with his cowardice.

What was this? Someone was shaking his hand and congratulating him. In a daze, Serge looked up to see a cluster of faces around the door. Then there was a muffled cheer as he staggered to his feet, lurched toward the opening, and stepped shakily out of the container. Wonderingly he looked round the room. With a catch in his breath he realized that the other eleven cabins had been removed, and that his own was standing alone. Had he won? Had he stuck it out longest? Serge could hardly believe it.

It was true. Boronoff came pushing through the little crowd. He smiled at the young man and extended his hand in congratulation.

"You have lasted longest, Comrade Smyslov," the scientist said. "So I suppose it will be you who will make the journey to our satellite."

Serge's brain was still not functioning properly, and the import of the leader's words did not immediately strike him.

"How long—have I—been inside?" he managed to gasp to the men around him.

"Twelve days, two hours, fifty-six minutes," someone called from the back of the crowd. "You've won by over two days."

HE'D WON! So he hadn't disgraced himself after all. A tremendous feeling of relief crept over him. So they didn't know how hard it had been. No matter, it was over now. But why were Boronoff and the others looking at him so curiously? Then something seemed to click in his head. He understood now the words he had heard the professor use. His face flushed, then went pale and flushed again as their significance dawned upon him. Was he pleased? Was he frightened? Was he excited? Serge just didn't know. All he knew with any certainty was—*he was going to the moon.*

CHAPTER 4

No one would have guessed that Sir George Benson had voted wholeheartedly to have Frayling appointed director of Operation Columbus. The two men faced each other with the same cold hostility that had characterized their relationship during their previous association. It was as if the intervening period of friendship had never existed.

"I happen to know that young Godfrey wishes to be selected," Benson was telling the director. "Personally, however, I think he should not be considered."

"And why not? If he wants to risk his neck again, let him. Someone has to go, and he's had more experience of space travel than anyone living," Frayling said with the hint of a sneer.

"Frayling, I'm asking you not to consider Chris for this venture, even if he is foolish enough to volunteer. He mustn't tempt Providence a third time," Sir George said earnestly.

"That's his own lookout," Frayling retorted. "If he formally volunteers, and is found to be the most suitable applicant—which is quite likely—then he'll be chosen."

"I must tell you that I shall try to dissuade him," Benson said candidly, as he hobbled out of Sir Leo's office.

"Now look here, Chris," Sir George said, "you must put this idea out of your head at once. It's not to be thought of."

They were sitting in Sir George's flat, late that same evening. Benson had sent an urgent message to his young friend that he wanted to see him, and Chris had traveled up to London from Cambridge, wondering what it was all about. Within a very short time he knew. Without mincing words, Benson told Chris that it would be sheer stupidity for him to risk his life again.

"You've been very, very lucky, Chris, and you can't expect it to continue. Surely you can see that," Sir George pointed out. "I fulfilled my part of our light-hearted little pact by informing Sir Leo of your crazy desire, but I also told him that I would try to dissuade you from the idea."

Chris's affection and admiration for Sir George were boundless. He hated to upset his friend like this, but he knew that, cost what it might, he had to complete his life's work. To set foot on Earth's satellite had now become more important to him than anything else. He must go, despite Uncle George's wishes. Even though he had barely escaped with his life on two former adventures, he must offer himself for this final crowning achievement. He sighed as he told his friend that he would—he must—volunteer for the lunar journey.

"I wish I could disclaim all responsibility for this crazy notion of yours," the scientist said bitterly, "but I can't escape the stark fact that it was I who persuaded you to go on your first flight in a rocket. If it had been someone else, you wouldn't be here now causing me all this worry."

"Perhaps that person would have wanted to go on this trip as much as I do," the youth pointed out.

"Not on your life," Benson declared firmly. "Anyone else would have enough sense not to risk his neck again. Only you, Chris, would be foolish enough—or brave enough—to want another go."

"I can't help it," Chris said. "I know I've got to."

"Well, did you dissuade your friend?" Frayling asked Benson next day.

Sir George's face was pale. "No," he snapped. "The young fool won't see sense. He insists on volunteering."

"Then he probably will go," Frayling said evenly. "That is, if he can stand the tests."

At a full meeting of the committee that afternoon, discussion centered on Christopher Godfrey's volunteering to play the all-important role in Operation Columbus. The tremendous advantage of his previous experience was pointed out. Then someone made the point of the desirability of a young man from one of the other co-operating countries making the space trip. After all, this was an international undertaking. After a long discussion it was finally decided to let Chris offer his services together with a suitable young American and that whichever of the two passed all the tests would be selected. With that Frayling seemed content and Sir George had, perforce, to be, too.

Chris's letter formally placing himself at the disposal of the Columbus Committee was received without emotion by Sir Leo Frayling the next morning. He read it to the full committee, which confirmed the director's proposal to accept the offer conditionally. Dr. Rosenberg promised to present the name of the American nominee within a week. Both young men, it was decided, should get their training at the newly organized Department of Space Medicine in the Royal Aeronautical Establishment at Farnborough.

When Chris received the letter from the committee he was a little disturbed at the news of a rival. Somehow he had never doubted that he would be chosen to make the flight. It had seemed to be the consummation of his life for which all his other adventures had been the preliminary steps. In the possibility that he might not be selected for Operation Columbus he thought he could see the hand of Uncle George. He sighed at the thought of a rift between his friend and himself.

That night Chris wrote a long letter to another old friend of his, Wing Commander Greatrex, whom everyone called "Whiskers." Whiskers had been his close and constant companion through all the perils of the past, and it was Whiskers who had saved Chris's life when his first rocket was crashing helplessly to Earth. In the letter he tried to explain the compulsion he felt to venture into space once more.

He told of the painful scene with Uncle George, and how, in spite of it, he had written to the committee and had now heard that he would be considered along with a young American. Chris implored the Wing Commander to try and get his point of view over to Benson, for he hated this estrangement between them.

Next morning Chris was relieved to receive his instructions to report to Farnborough. It would be good to get back to this establishment where he'd received training twice before. Would any of his former acquaintances still be there? he wondered. And what about his American rival? What would he be like? Would the two of them soon be engaged in a bitter struggle to be chosen?

At ever-changing Farnborough, new devices were constantly being constructed to test and torture the human frame. Always the scientists and doctors could think up fresh means of simulating the physical conditions found in space. Chris's own experience had been of use to those ingenious men.

Chris strode up to the main gate, his blue canvas bag swinging jauntily at his side. The full resources of this famous establishment would, he knew, be used to fit him—or his rival—for the hazards of lunar landing.

Ten minutes later, after a number of phone calls from the guard room, an old friend came to take Chris from the care of the flight sergeant on guard. It was Squadron Leader Lambert, who had been responsible for conditioning Chris for his last adventure. The two shook hands cordially, and the officer led him away to the administrative buildings.

"How many new gadgets have you thought up now?" Chris asked as they walked along.

"Oh, a few." His friend smiled. "There are still your old pals, the centrifuge and the 'coffin,' but now you'll have the compression chamber and the 'fridge' thrown in. All of them will be a bit tougher than before. I'm afraid you'll be up against a much stiffer job this time, Chris, and when you get to the moon you'll be doing far more complicated tasks than when you were just putting down a marker beacon. So your training here will be that much harder. You'll have to do many difficult things in the artificial conditions we'll create."

"That's all right," Chris answered sturdily. "I'll try to take all you can give me. All I hope is that the other chap doesn't come out of it as well as I do. I've got to beat him to this job."

"I hope you do, Chris; but of course, you'll both have exactly the same treatment."

"Anyhow, I'm going on this trip," Chris said grimly.

Chris spent the rest of the day settling into his new quarters and wandering round the vast collection of buildings and research equipment. One of his first visits was to the centrifuge, to see that huge machine that can hurl a man round and round at many times the acceleration of Earth's gravity. Chris had had many turns in the monster and he had no fear of it at all. Things were different when he came to the "coffin"— a small chamber inside a larger building.

In the restricted space of the simulated rocket cabin

he had had to spend many terrifying hours. This part of his former training had nearly defeated him, until Sir Leo Frayling had decreed that he was to be anesthetized, as the first research animals had been. This had helped him to overcome his claustrophobia and to complete his rocket journey successfully. He had never been in a compression chamber or a refrigerator, though, and he wondered what they would be like.

The following morning Chris wrote a long letter to his aunt, explaining to her that he hoped soon to be away on another rocket flight. By this time, he was sure, Mrs. Ingall would be resigned to this peculiar propensity of her nephew's. That she would be worried about him he knew, but he hoped she'd remember that he'd come safely out of similar adventures.

Lambert told Chris that his training couldn't start until his American rival arrived, since both contenders for the flight were to have exactly equal training and tests. Godfrey's only advantage over the American would be his previous experience. So Chris must pass the next few days as best he could.

"Oh, and one other thing," Lambert went on. "This American lad will have a friend, bodyguard, companion, or what you will, in the person of a U. S. Air Force major, and rumor has it that you'll get a nurse-maid too. Someone you know very well."

"Not Whiskers?" Chris asked.

"None other than Wing Commander Greatrex himself." The Squadron Leader grinned.

Chris was delighted at the news. He thought of Whiskers as a close and dear friend, second only to Uncle George. What fun it would be to see him again! And Whiskers, who would report for duty next day, would be glad, no doubt, to escape from the routine duties which irked a former fighter pilot.

As Chris wandered about the establishment, or idly turned the pages of magazines in the lounge, he thought more and more about the young American who was to share his training. It would be interesting to have a competitor in the fantastic tests he would have to undergo, but the possibility that his rival might fare better than he dismayed him a little. Somehow he felt he wasn't going to like this young man from the States.

It was a happy reunion between Chris and Greatrex. Chris was delighted to see his old friend again and to hear his boisterous, happy laugh. The famous mustache had lost none of its bristle or mobility, and Chris found himself watching it with the same fascination as before. Whiskers was full of questions about his young friend's life at the university, and about Mrs. Ingall, his aunt. On his part, Chris asked about Mrs. Whiskers and the lusty infant who everyone declared was the living image of his father—except of course, for the mustache.

When the preliminaries were over, the two friends began to talk more seriously about the project that had brought them together. Chris repeated all he had written about the irresistible urge he felt to complete his life's task by landing on the moon. He told of the painful interview he'd had with Sir George and of how sorry he felt to be going against the scientist's wishes. He admitted that Sir George had been very fair in presenting his name to Sir Leo. Whiskers asked Christopher earnestly if he was fully aware of the risks he was going to undertake, and of what he was doing. The reply was so emphatic that the Wing Commander no longer had any doubts.

"Very well then, Chris," he said, looking the young man keenly in the face. "I'll do all I can to help you and to persuade old Benny to accept the situation with good grace. Of course," he went on, "it's possible the American laddie might—"

"Look, Whiskers," Chris interrupted earnestly. "I've just got to beat that Yankee. I must go. I must!"

"Oh well, we'll worry about that when the time comes," Whiskers said more cheerfully. "If there's anything I can do to clinch the matter—short of hobbling the opposition—I'll do it. Now come and show me where I hang my hat."

As he had done so many times before, Greatrex set about cheering up his friend. Soon Chris was laughing heartily with the irrepressible Wing Commander.

Later that day Chris and Squadron Leader Lambert conducted Whiskers around the establishment. In spite of himself, Whiskers shuddered a little at the "coffin" which he remembered so vividly. When he was shown the fearsome new gadgets he said, "If all these tortures don't scare the Yank, I'll be surprised."

CHAPTER 5

Morrison Kant, the young American with whom Chris was to compete, arrived three days later with Major Simmonds, his companion. The Squadron Leader brought the news to young Godfrey and his friend. Immediately Chris was impatient to meet his rival.

"What's he like? Does he look tough?" he asked Lambert.

But the Air Force doctor smilingly refused to enlighten him. "You'll be meeting him yourself in about half an hour," he explained.

The wait seemed interminable. At last Chris, with Whiskers following behind, was led to the office of the establishment's commanding officer. Air Commodore Wilson invited them to come in.

Inside the door, Chris's eyes swept instantly to the young American, who was looking at him just as keenly. The two young men studied each other with an intensity that made them oblivious to the other occupants of the room.

Kant was a tall, well-built young man, perhaps a year older than Chris. His fair hair was crew cut.

Lively brown eyes lit up a strong lean face. Rather hesitantly he flashed Chris a smile and held out his hand in greeting. His face flushing slightly, Godfrey responded with a firm handshake. Did he like this American or not?

"Morrison Kant—Christopher Godfrey," the C. O. introduced them, and for a long ten seconds the rivals looked into each other's eyes.

"Major Simmonds—Wing Commander Greatrex," the introductions went on, and then Chris turned his gaze to the American officer. For a moment one would have thought that the pair from the States were father and son, or—perhaps more accurately—two brothers. For the major had the same tall figure, the same hairstyle, the same facial contours as his younger compatriot. Only his eyes, a definite blue, were different from Kant's.

What his feelings about the Americans were at that precise moment, Chris didn't know. He wanted to dislike them both intensely, but their cheerful grins and friendly greetings made the process difficult. A flood of shame swept over Chris a few moments later as he realized how curt his own words had been. He was about to speak to young Kant when an interruption came in the form of a white-coated waiter carrying a tray laden with glasses of sherry. The C. O. invited his guests to join him in a drink, and the first awkward moments of the encounter were over.

"You've been up in a rocket twice, haven't you?" Morrison Kant was eagerly asking Christopher.

"Er—yes," Chris stammered diffidently. Then he added, more firmly, "And if I can, I want to go up again."

Morrison's grin became wider.

"We'll have to see about that! But there's no reason why we shouldn't be friends, is there? We'll be seeing a lot of each other, I guess. My friends call me Morrey. Are you called Chris?"

Chris nodded. He badly wanted to turn on his heel and walk away, but good manners compelled him to be polite.

"What part of America do you come from?" he asked.

"A little place called Peterborough, in New Hampshire," Morrey replied. "Do you live in London?"

"No. I'm from a small town called Wolverton, though I'm at Cambridge University at the moment," Chris explained.

"That's swell! Two of my friends were there a couple of years back. I saw some movies they took of the colleges. Fine old buildings! I entered M. I. T.— Massachusetts Institute of Technology—last fall. Wonderful place, though it hasn't the history of Cambridge. You know, Chris, you're lucky to live in a country with all the traditions that Britain has."

"I thought you Americans made fun of us for being proud of the past and not progressive enough about the future," Chris said in surprise.

"Don't you believe it! We've a pretty high opinion of you in the States—even if we find you a bit stuffy in some things." Morrey said this with a disarming grin.

The older men were standing in a group a little distance away. As they sipped their drinks, Major Simmonds asked if the training program had been drawn up. The C. O. nodded, and said that now both young men were present it would go into operation at once.

The weeks that followed were full of activity. The two young men experienced the whole gamut of tests and tortures that the establishment could provide. Chris was soon at home in his old friend the centrifuge— that huge machine that whirled him round and round in a tiny gondola at a fantastic speed. He became, as before, quite accustomed to the terrific strain on his body caused by the high acceleration.

On this Morrey didn't fare so well. Bravely clenching his teeth, the young American submitted to the painful and terrifying experience gamely enough, but Chris noted the nervous sweat on his forehead each time he was due for a spell in the machine. Yet he never complained or hesitated. Whether this pleased Chris or not, he didn't quite know. Part of him wanted the American to confess himself beaten and to withdraw from this strange contest, while another part could not help but admire Morrey's courage.

In the little chamber built to resemble the cabin of the rocket, the positions were reversed. The two young men had to spend long spells in this confined space to accustom them to the sixty-hour journey one of them would make in similar surroundings. Chris found his sessions in the "coffin" almost unendurable, while Morrey managed them quite unperturbed. It was a relief to the young Britisher to know that whoever was sent in the rocket would be anesthetized, as he had been before. This was primarily to reduce the oxygen consumption to a minimum, but it also enabled Chris to conquer his claustrophobia.

Both young men had to spend many hours in a decompression chamber surrounded by an almost perfect vacuum such as it was expected they would encounter on the lunar surface. The specially designed space suits they wore made movement difficult, and much practice was required before they could perform the tasks that were set them.

Two more chambers had to be entered. One was freezing cold and the other extremely hot. Both the space suits and their wearers must be able to withstand these extremes of temperature, common on the moon. Finally, both Morrey and Chris had frequent flights in high-speed aircraft which performed a special maneuver to reproduce the conditions of free fall. Though these weightless spells were of less than a minute's duration, they served to introduce young Kant to this strange experience.

During these strenuous but exciting weeks, Sir George Benson visited the establishment only twice. On each occasion Chris felt the gulf that divided them. Any conversation was as brief as possible, and Chris was left with a heavy heart. Yet he knew that Benson gave close attention to the smallest detail of Operation Columbus, and that Simmonds, Greatrex, and Lambert had to furnish Benson, as well as Frayling, with constant and detailed reports.

On the opposite side of the world, in Woomera, a little township created on the fringe of the South Australian desert, Britain and Australia had built up a gigantic testing range for rockets. Away to the north stretched fifteen hundred miles of virtually uninhabited territory—uninhabited, that is, except for a few aborigines and the crews of numerous tracking stations.

For years the two governments had been developing Woomera. Now it had every imaginable facility and device required for rocket launching, rivaling in every way the great American base at Cape Canaveral. In addition, all its tracking stations were on land which, for accuracy, was preferable to stations aboard ships. It was from Woomera that Chris's two epic launchings had been made. Now the other co-operating countries had once more agreed readily to the use of the Anglo-Australian base for Operation Columbus.

Sir George Benson was, of course, delighted that his Research Establishment had been selected again as the focal point of a great international effort to conquer the unknown. His staff, augmented by a large contingent from the United States and smaller ones from France and West Germany, had swung into enthusiastic action. The deputy director, Mr. W. H. R. G. Gillanders—Billy, to his friends—was rapidly welding the different nationals into one great team. This was not a difficult task with scientists and technicians who respected each other's achievements.

Speedy jet planes shuttled Columbus Committee

members backward and forward around the globe as occasion demanded. In one particularly hectic fortnight Frayling and Benson had journeyed from London to Woomera and back twice. Rarely a week passed that did not see one or both of them, with other committee colleagues, making what was becoming almost a humdrum trip. Never had the Rocket Research Establishment, occupied now by the foremost scientists and technicians of the West, worked with such concentrated effort. Even in the little township there was an air of suppressed excitement as preparations went on round the clock to assemble the giant four-stage rocket.

Gillanders worked tirelessly, rarely snatching more than a few hours for sleep in the bungalow where he lived with his wife and daughter. As Sir George's deputy, the task of detailed administration fell on his shoulders. Arranging accommodations for the American, French, and German contingents was a formidable task in itself. Yet this was only one of the many extra things Billy had to do.

Others included the supervision of the construction and equipment of extra tracking stations; the installation of a gigantic radio aerial, shaped like a spider's web, on which it was hoped to pick up the weak radio signals from the lunar explorer; and the storage of vast quantities of the dangerously powerful new fuels with which the rocket stages were to be charged.

Mrs. Gillanders and her daughter Betty were old friends of Chris Godfrey's. He had stayed with them before his previous rocket journeys. They, too, wanted Chris to avoid the fearful risks of a third journey into space. During his flying visits to the establishment, Benson often stayed with the Gillanders, and they soon learned how he felt about Chris's determination to go to the moon. Betty and Helen, her mother, thought Chris had gone clean crazy, but Billy wasn't so sure.

Back at Farnborough, the training of the two young

men was nearing its final stages. Both had survived all the tests satisfactorily, and the hour of decision was drawing near. Often Chris found himself praying silently that the choice might fall on him, yet he had to admit Morrey Kant's fitness for the job. The energy, good humor, and enthusiasm of the young American had overcome Godfrey's early dislike, and the two contenders for the journey into the unknown had become firm friends.

Sir Leo interviewed the young men frequently, both separately and together. He studied closely the reports of the doctors and psychologists who had been responsible for the program. Sir George Benson had made no further appeal to the chief scientist not to choose Christopher, knowing full well that to do so would be useless. It might even, perhaps, have the opposite effect from what was intended.

When Sir George requested an interview, Frayling knew it could scarcely be about Operation Columbus, as the committee had concluded a very full review of the project barely an hour before. With some curiosity the director motioned Benson into a chair and waited for him to speak.

"You will shortly be choosing the person to make the voyage," Benson began, "and it's about that I wanted to speak. I want you to know, Frayling, that I've withdrawn any opposition I had to young Godfrey's being chosen. You know how I felt at first. But in view of his strong desire, I've put aside my own misgivings. Now I am determined to do all I can to ensure his selection. I thought that if you knew this you might be more inclined in his favor."

"Indeed. And what makes you think that?" Sir Leo asked frigidly. "Only one thing will influence my decision, and that is—which of those two young men is most suitable. I'm surprised that you imagined any intervention of yours could influence me, Benson."

"Quite," Sir George replied evenly. "Though of

course I can only contribute my intimate knowledge of Christopher to the data on which you will choose. Whatever may be the qualities of the American boy, Godfrey is still the only one who has proved his courage and psychological suitability under the actual conditions he will meet. Although every effort is made at Farnborough to simulate as nearly as possible the physical strains of space flight, the subject knows all along that the conditions are artificial, that they are carefully prepared, and that he is in little or no danger. They cannot, therefore, have the same value as actual experience of totally unknown conditions, such as Christopher has twice survived. Be sensible, Frayling, and face this incontestable fact. I know the lad can do the job, and now I want him to be allowed to try."

"Is that all you have to say, Benson? Then be good enough to waste no more of my time. Good day." The chief scientist's voice grated coldly as Sir George stood up, shrugged, and made his slow way toward the door. He did not see the hard glitter in Frayling's eyes.

Morrey and Chris were both summoned to Sir Leo's office in London. So this was it!

The two young men had known that Sir Leo's decision was imminent. They had both completed their tasks; they had both stood up to all that Farnborough could devise; they were both desperately anxious to face the perils that lay ahead. For most of the car journey they were silent, each wondering what the outcome would be; each praying silently that he was the one to be chosen. An equally serious Wing Commander Greatrex and Major Simmonds accompanied them.

As the little party approached Sir Leo's office, Chris felt pretty ghastly. He could see that Morrey was feeling the strain, too. It would be untrue to say that he wished his American friend luck, for he wanted to go in that rocket now more than ever. He could not bear to think what he would do if Morrey were chosen.

The little party strode along the echoing corridor until they came in the fateful door. With a restraint altogether strange to him, Whiskers tapped on the panel.

"Come in," Sir Leo's voice called. The four of them stepped into the room.

Without even asking them to sit down, the scientist began to address them in his most impersonal manner. He reviewed the training that each young man had had, and the care that had been taken in devising their tasks. He had studied all the reports, had given a great deal of thought to the matter, and was now in a position to announce his selection.

He paused for a moment to stare keenly at the two young men standing before him. Two haggard anxious faces gazed into his own, trying hard to read what lay behind those steely gray eyes. For Chris time seemed to stand still, with only the thudding of his pulse to mark its passage. His knees were weak and shaky, and he could feel a light film of moisture on his face.

"I have decided," Sir Leo Frayling announced, "that the person to be launched will be Morrison Kant!"

CHAPTER 6

To Chris the words came almost as a physical blow.

Morrison Kant! It wasn't possible!

He felt the strong arm of Wing Commander Great-rex encircle his shoulders and with gentle pressure guide him out of the room. In the corridor, Whiskers kept his arm around his stunned young friend. A gently affectionate squeeze conveyed a wealth of meaning to Chris, smitten now with a fear that he would break down and howl like a child. With a supreme effort he stilled his quivering chin and wiped away the hot smarting tears that had somehow sprung to his eyes. Only then had he the courage to look old Whiskers in the face.

Greatrex was almost as upset as his friend. Memories of their long association came flooding into Chris's mind, and with them a sense of guilt. Somehow he'd let Whiskers down. Somehow he'd fallen short in the tests. Somehow Morrey had beaten him to the post, and his previous experience counted for nothing.

The thought of the American shook Chris to the core. Morrison was to go in the rocket; he'd won the fateful contest between them. And he, Chris, had walked out of the office without a word of congratulation to his friend! He turned to the understanding Whiskers and, his face working painfully, managed to gasp out, "Morrey! I—haven't congratulated him!"

"All right, Chris. Another time will do." Greatrex spoke soothingly as he urged his stricken friend along the corridor.

Dumbly Chris stumbled forward. Near the entrance to the building a uniformed commissionaire handed a sealed envelope to the Wing Commander, which he opened. Inside was a single sheet of paper carrying brief typewritten instructions. Chris was to collect his things from Farnborough and return to his former occupation. All connection with Operation Columbus was terminated forthwith.

So that was it! He was finished, discarded, useless! Bitterness welled up inside Chris as his friend explained as gently as possible what the instructions were. As he sat in the taxi which Greatrex had called, Chris felt himself tossed like a cork on a sea of conflicting emotions. The crushing disappointment of his rejection jostled with intense anger at the cavalier fashion in which it had been done. Regret at his failure to congratulate Morrison alternated with bewilderment about the future. What would he do now? Return to the university? It was unthinkable, in the mood he was in.

Automatically, guided by his sympathetic friend, Christopher made the journey back to Farnborough. There, with heavy hearts, the pair, still mainly silent, went to Chris's quarters—the room he had left with such high hopes only a few hours before. As he was pushing some clothing into a case, a knock came on the door, and Lambert stepped inside.

Whether he knew already, or whether he read the situation in the somber faces of the other two, Lambert didn't say. He came over to Chris to say how sorry he was. Chris managed to force a strained smile in reply.

"You're coming to our place for a few days," Whiskers said firmly as he led his companion out of the main gates. "It'll give you time to get things straight. Come on."

Without protest Chris followed, and that evening found him in the Greatrex's comfortable home, with Sylvia fussing over him and baby Alec insisting on his attention. Gradually he began to relax in the warm, friendly atmosphere, though inwardly he felt as if some part of him had died. He went quietly to bed that night, knowing he wouldn't sleep.

Staring ahead into the darkness, he recalled the scene in Sir Leo's office and heard once more the coldly spoken words that had sounded the death knell for all his hopes and ambitions. Wouldn't Uncle George be pleased! As this thought crossed his mind, Chris had a further shattering idea. Perhaps, after all, Uncle George had succeeded in influencing Sir Leo. Was it his intervention that had persuaded the director to choose his rival? Had his greatest friend managed to prevent him from fulfilling his life's ultimate aim?

Chris fought unsuccessfully against this growing suspicion. For what seemed countless ages he lay staring miserably into the darkness. Then, for some reason, he remembered that in his acute distress he'd forgotten to say his prayers. He climbed out of bed and spent a long time on his knees. Afterward things seemed a little better, and within minutes he was asleep.

Next morning Sylvia Greatrex was pleased to see her young guest, though still subdued, looking much better. Whiskers went out of his way to cheer him up and, to some extent, succeeded. After breakfast Christopher asked the Wing Commander if he could possibly see Morrey Kant, for he'd like to show the American that he had no personal resentment against him for his success.

Whiskers promised he'd have a session on the telephone and try to fix a meeting. At lunchtime he was able to tell Chris that Morrey and Major Simmonds would meet them that afternoon in a little cafe in Farnborough which they had all used frequently. The two Americans were to be flown out to Woomera at dawn the next day.

The meeting was an embarrassment to both young men. Chris stammered his apologies and congratulations. Morrey, far from trying to triumph over his unsuccessful opponent, acted guilty for having robbed the other of his greatest ambition.

"Give my love to Mr. and Mrs. Gillanders and Betty. I know you'll be very happy with them." Chris smiled bravely.

"Sure wish you were coming too, Chris," the American said earnestly.

The two older men also exchanged farewells, and the little party moved toward the door. They had been in the cafe for not quite ten minutes. Outside, there were brief handshakes, and then the Britons turned one way and the Americans another.

Late that evening Christopher was vainly trying to look interested in a television program when the Greatrex doorbell rang. A few seconds later the door opened and Sir George Benson came in, leaning on his canes.

For a moment Chris stood still. He could feel the color leaving his face. Sir George stepped forward with hand outstretched.

"Hello, Chris," he said, waiting for the other to shake his hand.

"Hello," Chris said in a still, small voice. Automatically he shook hands with Sir George, who looked at him keenly, oblivious to the others in the room.

"I want you to believe that I am truly sorry about this, Chris," he said.

For a moment Chris paused, almost as if he were about to turn away. As he hesitated, Benson went on.

"It's true, lad. I've changed my mind, though of course it's too late now."

"But—when did you do that?"

The scientist looked extremely uncomfortable.

"I've a confession to make, Chris," he explained. "Just before he made his decision, I called on Frayling. Knowing how he feels about me, I asked him to choose you. I banked on that being sufficient to turn the scales against you. Then I realized I'd done a pretty low trick, and that set me thinking it all out again. My opposition to your participation was wholly selfish, based solely on my affection for you. That's—that's all over now. Not my affection," he added quickly. "The opposition, I mean."

Chris didn't speak. His thoughts were far too jumbled. It was rather embarrassing to have Benson speaking like this. A pity he hadn't changed his mind a bit earlier. Then, as Chris realized what this explanation must have cost Sir George, he was filled with shame. Impulsively he put out his hand again and clasped that of the scientist.

"The tragedy is," Benson went on, "that I don't know whether my intervention had any influence on Frayling's choice. I suppose I shall never know whether or not that strange man turned you down because of me."

"It doesn't matter now, Uncle George," Chris assured him. "Still, I'm glad you've told me this."

The tension was eased, the restraint gone; only disappointment remained. Whiskers took advantage of the improved situation to create an almost party atmosphere. His happy laugh, his sense of fun, his amazing store of stories, all helped along the process of healing. Sylvia's quieter charm helped, too. When Sir George took his leave just short of midnight, he and Christopher were back on their old footing.

"Ah, well, that's that," Chris told himself with a mental shrug as he lay in bed that night. "It's no use crying over spilt milk. Morrey's off to Woomera, and tomorrow I must think of my future."

As he was having breakfast next morning, Chris did give one regretful thought to the young American who, at that moment, must be halfway across Europe on his journey to Australia. Then he turned his mind with grim determination to deciding his own future course. It wasn't going to be easy to return to his studies at the university. He felt like many of the fellows he'd known in his grammar-school days, who, having failed an exam, had to return to school for another year. Some of those chaps, Chris remembered, returned full of bravado, as if they didn't care. But, deep down, he knew they felt the situation just as keenly as the others did.

Yes, he'd have to return to his studies, for without them he would never get that coveted appointment with Uncle George at the Rocket Research Establishment. Having made his decision, he was anxious to act upon it without delay. The sooner he was back in the old routine, the sooner he would recover from his bitter disappointment.

At breakfast he told Whiskers what he had decided, and he was strengthened in his resolve by Greatrex's warm approval. He called Benson, who offered to accompany him back to Cambridge that morning. Chris gladly accepted the offer and enjoyed the ride there with Sir George. The atmosphere between them was no longer strained; it was like old times. In a few days Chris was making such frantic efforts to catch up lost time, to copy notes of lectures he'd missed, to absorb new work, that he was not only fully occupied but had almost forgotten his frustration. Almost, but not quite.

The Gillanders family were disappointed that instead of their friend Christopher they were to entertain a stranger. Betty vowed she would dislike him on sight, but a stern warning from her father drew from the girl a promise that she would treat the American as a welcome guest.

When he arrived, Morrey Kant's friendly grin soon broke down all opposition. If Betty and her mother couldn't have Chris to stay with them, then this attractive young American would do. When he was not engaged on training or instruction Morrey went on long walks or rides with Betty. While the army of engineers, scientists and technicians worked unceasingly on the lunar rocket, for the young people the time passed pleasantly enough.

Due to pressure of work on Operation Columbus in London, Sir Leo Frayling had not been at Woomera since Morrey arrived. His absence contributed in no small way to the general air of gay excitement as the rocket neared completion. Billy Gillanders often declared that an atmosphere of gloom settled over the establishment as soon as Frayling's plane crossed the equator. Now, with Sir Leo still away and with a free day on his hands, Morrison and Betty galloped away joyously for a long day's ride. The saddlebags were loaded with food and drink and the young couple were in high spirits.

It was nearly midnight. Chris put away his notes wearily. The going was harder than he had anticipated, but at last he seemed to be catching up on the lectures he had missed while he was at Farnborough. Perhaps in another week his studies would be at the stage in which he had left them. He sighed unconsciously as he thought of what might have been. Perhaps it was because he was so weary that thoughts of Operation Columbus, of Woomera, and of all his friends out there, came flooding back.

For days he'd resisted the temptation to indulge in vain regrets, but now he sat back in his chair, eyes closed, thinking, thinking, thinking. With angry shame he brushed away the tear that had somehow rolled down his cheek.

Christopher sat up with a start. Someone was knocking at his door. Vaguely he had heard a car stop outside, but had been too preoccupied to pay any attention. Now, as the knock was repeated, he got up to answer the door. Who could it be at this time of night?

Uncle George!

Chris gaped in astonishment. It required an effort to gather his wits sufficiently to invite his caller inside. As he stepped into the lighted hall Chris could see that Benson was laboring under intense excitement. The room door closed behind them and the younger man turned expectantly toward the scientist for an explanation. He hadn't long to wait.

"Chris," Sir George burst out, "pack your bags. You're off to Woomera. Your friend Kant has fallen off a horse and broken a leg. Frayling sent me down as soon as the news came through. You're to make the journey to the moon after all, my lad. And you're starting for Australia tonight!"

CHAPTER 7

"We know that the Western imperialists are straining every nerve to get ahead of the Soviet Union," the commissar was saying. "Our agents tell us that their launching will be made from Woomera in Australia. The Soviet Union is determined that Earth's satellite shall not fall under Western rule. You are therefore required to take all steps necessary to prevent the Anglo-American group from obtaining any information from this new area of our influence."

Serge Smyslov first listened silently. Getting a thorough political indoctrination was an important part of his training. Apart from glowing accounts of Russian history and Communist achievement, this usually took the form of sustained vilification of all things Western. Different commissars would lecture him for hours, often repeating one another almost word for word. The susceptible young man was thoroughly convinced as to the evil designs of the imperialists and of the youth they would be sending as their advance guard.

Sometimes Serge would speak to some of the scientists with whom he came into contact. It was very strange, he found, that these men never spoke against the Western world. They listened silently whenever they received their political lecture, but he got the impression that they did not altogether accept what they were being told. Dr. Boronoff in particular seemed pro-Western—a result, it was remarked, of his recent association with British and American scientists. Nothing could be greater proof of his high standing in Soviet science than the fact that he had not been purged for his leanings—so far.

The minitank functioned perfectly. Serge had numerous opportunities to put it through its paces. Driven by special batteries, it was able to travel for several days without recharging. In front were a pair of mechanical "hands," and the young Russian became adept in their use. On the moon he would employ them to collect samples of rock and of various types of lunar surface and, above all, fragments of the artificial domes which were of such mysterious origin.

Inside the little tank would be a whole array of instruments to record temperature, pressure of any atmosphere, radiation, and impact of micro-meteorites. A film camera would operate automatically while the vehicle was in motion. There was also a cannon-like tube from which small rockets could be fired to break off lumps of rock. A powerful two-way radio would enable Serge to contact his headquarters and to receive his orders.

According to the careful plans the Soviet scientists had worked out, Serge was to spend two days exploring as much as possible of the moon's surface. Then, after no more than fifty hours, he must return to his rocket, seal himself inside, and restart the motors for his journey back to Earth.

All these things Serge practiced, even to launching himself in a rocket to simulate the take-off from the moon. From the rocket the compartment carrying the minitank would be recovered by parachute—an expensive but effective method of training. With character-

istic thoroughness the Russian scientists prepared the
young man for the task that lay ahead. Every possible
eventuality was thought of and the action necessary
to meet it carefully worked out and tested. Serge felt
he could do his job in his sleep. He was full of confidence, his old secret fear buried in the deepest recesses
of his subconscious mind.

The young Russian never quite knew when the
idea was first suggested to him, but in some subtle
manner he became aware that he must destroy the
imperialist emissary if he should get that opportunity.
Never must the Western war-mongers be allowed to
colonize the Queen of the Night. They must be warned
in unmistakable terms that the moon was to become a
Soviet Socialist Republic, and that no interference from
the capitalists would be tolerated. If necessary the
rocket gun could be used to blast more than pieces of
lunar rock!

In strictest secrecy, with security precautions as
rigorous as any taken in wartime, preparations for the
launching moved toward a climax. The precise date
and time were fixed. Serge was as ready as he would
ever be. The rocket was completed and fueled. Now
the First Secretary of the Communist Party came to
shake the young man's hand, and, on behalf of the
Soviet Union, to wish him success for his journey.
For the next few days the eyes of all Russians would
be turned toward the skies, for as soon as the rocket
was safely away the full blast of Soviet propaganda
would be unleashed, telling all the world of the glorious
Soviet venture.

With all the excitement of last-minute preparations,
the visit of the Soviet leaders, and the final sessions of
political instruction, Serge had little time to take stock
of his own feelings. All he knew was that it was the
greatest possible honor that he should have been
selected to bear the Communist flag and to plant it for
the first time in a New World. Let the imperialists do

their worst, he was resolved that Russia—and she alone —should receive the vital information which would permit a full-scale landing to follow. . . .

In this ecstasy of devotion to his Communist ideals the young Russian experienced only rarely the mysterious doubts that arose from deep within him. These were quickly forgotten in the flood of final instructions and ultimate tasks before the launching. So dawned the day that was to witness the great Soviet advance into the universe.

Some two hours before the time chosen for the launching, all the personnel engaged on that vast project who could be spared from their immediate tasks assembled around the firing apron. From a rostrum at the foot of the tall, gleaming rocket, high Communist officials addressed the gathering. For almost an hour one after another poured words into the battery of microphones that carried their voices to the extremities of the crowd, as well as to those scientists and technicians who could not leave their posts.

After a long harangue the First Secretary came to the climax of his address. With almost theatrical effect, he declared that the gigantic witness to Soviet achievement that stood beside him should be christened "Lenin," after that great architect of Communism. Thunderous applause followed.

The speechmaking was over; the politicians had withdrawn to a safe distance; the engineers and scientists had gone to their posts. Serge was assisted into the minitank nestling in the top section of the rocket. The hands of the control-room clock were steadily approaching zero hour.

Lying on the couch he would occupy during the period of acceleration, Serge was now alone. Apart from periodic reports he had to make over his radio, he was cut off from the world of his fellowmen. He would remain on that couch until the rocket reached its destination, the lunar crater called Plato. As he lay there awaiting the quivering that would be the first sign the rocket motors had been started, he felt those horrid fears begin to raise their ugly heads.

Sealed away from the sight of everyone, he was, without knowing it, lowering his defences against the black monster within him. What had he to combat it with? A conviction of the supremacy of Soviet science; a life of complete discipline and subservience to decrees of the Party; the certain knowledge of what would befall him if the project failed through any weakness of his.

At precisely 11:32 A.M. the firing switch was pulled. There was the inevitable pause while everyone wondered whether the rocket would explode or rise. It rose. From the billowing clouds of steam and smoke the rocket slowly emerged. Almost reluctantly, it seemed, it began slowly and ponderously to lift itself clear of its resting place.

Soon it could be seen right above the steelwork of the service gantry. A vicious tongue of flame roared from the tail. With incredible rapidity the rocket gained speed, becoming smaller and smaller in the sky. In a little over a minute from the time of firing, "Lenin" was a speck in the heavens. Then it had disappeared from sight.

Inside the rocket, Serge had held his breath as the fateful hour drew near. He was near panic when he felt the rocket begin to quiver. Before he could collect his senses he was pressed down tightly onto his seat by the terrific acceleration. It took all his willpower to hold back the cry of alarm that rose to his lips, but he did so, for the radio was on and he would be heard by those down below.

Had he known it, he could not have made a sound, for it would have been impossible for him to move his muscles under the terrific strain. How long the period of acceleration lasted Serge did not know. He soon slipped into merciful unconsciousness from which he recovered only when "Lenin" was coasting along on its path to the moon.

How good it was to be back in the middle of things again! As the plane sped through the night toward a new dawn, Chris lay back in his seat and thought of the last two hectic hours. On the other side of the aisle Uncle George lay with his eyes closed, though Chris knew he was not asleep. He had been true to his word. He had been as excited as Chris at the unexpected turn in his fortunes. It seemed Fate had decreed that his young friend should, after all, make the terrific journey. So be it! The two friends would be united once more in Operation Columbus.

There had been no time to dig out old Whiskers, but Sir George had left instructions for him to be told first thing in the morning to pack his bags and follow on the next plane. Then the old team would be complete, and Chris would be seeing his friends, the Gillanders family, into the bargain.

A few hours later the plane broke through the clouds and down below the passengers could see the white line of surf breaking on the Australian shore. In minutes, it seemed, they were coming in to land. Soon the Director of Research and his companion were boarding the smaller plane that would fly them to Woomera. Chris's excitement at meeting his friends grew as the plane flew on. Soon a jeep was rushing them to the Gillanders' white bungalow, where there were cordial greetings all around.

Among the happy friends there was one rather rueful figure—Morrison Kant, who was hobbling about with his left leg in a plaster cast. Chris thought he caught just a hint of bitter disappointment behind the grin with which Morrey greeted him, and he felt more than a little embarrassed as he fumbled for the right words to say.

"Sorry about your leg, Morrey," he burst out at

last, "though it would be silly to deny I'm pleased to be going on the rocket trip. Still, I wish it had been something else. I mean—that is, I don't mean I wish you'd broken something else, but—"

"That's all right." The American laughed. "I know what you mean, Chris. You're glad to be going, but you're sorry it had to be my accident that did it."

"Yes, that's it. I really am sorry about the leg. Will it be in a cast very long?"

"Too long," Morrey grumbled. "Though Mr. and Mrs. Gillanders have sure been mighty nice about everything. They've invited me to stay on here till I can go back home. Hope I'm here to see you blast off, Chris."

At this point Betty joined them, and the conversation turned to other subjects.

The next day Christopher had his first sight of the tall, shining giant that was to carry him into space. Out in the center of the concrete firing apron he saw the steel lattice-work of the service gantry, the huge movable structure that encased the rocket while it was being prepared. There were platforms at various levels, each with a group of men busily engaged on the final adjustments. The highest platform, smaller than the rest, was even with the nose cone. Chris could see the small aperture leading to the cabin in which he would make the flight. Everywhere men turned to greet him with a smile and a wave, for news had soon got round that Christopher Godfrey was to be the new pilot for Operation Columbus.

The rocket, which also bore the name of the famous explorer, was much larger than any Chris had seen. At the base, he was told, it was eight feet in diameter, and it towered nearly ninety feet into the air. Even the cabin in which he was to make the journey was more spacious than the cramped compartments he had known before. Certainly the instruments inside were more numerous, and much of his time during the next few days was spent in familiarizing himself with their uses and operation.

With Wing Commander Greatrex there also arrived Sir Leo and the other members of the Columbus Committee, their work in London now finished. On their arrival the Research Establishment took on an even more urgent air, for the days were running out. The launching must take place on the date arranged or at least another month would have to pass before another attempt could be made. Meanwhile, many of them wondered, what were the Russians doing?

Never had time passed so quickly for Chris. He had two sessions with the grim-faced Frayling to receive his final briefing. No one would have guessed from these interviews that a few weeks before the chief scientist and the young man had been on friendly terms. Now Sir Leo was the cold, hard, impersonal figure that Chris had disliked so much. Besides these meetings Chris spent many hours with various scientists, each a specialist in his own branch. He had periods of practice in wearing the heavy space suit that he was to wear on the moon. He knew that when he was actually walking on the rough lunar surface the weight would not be noticeable, because gravity was so much less there.

Twenty-four hours to go!

Chris learned from Sir George the actual time of the firing—at eleven-thirty the next morning. With Whiskers, Benson had spent as much time with Chris as his duties allowed. Now that only a day remained, the Director of Research felt many of his former misgivings return. It was only by a conscious effort that he kept them in check.

That last evening Chris and Betty Gillanders and Morrison Kant went for a quiet walk, the American hobbling along. None of them had much to say; each seemed busy with his or her thoughts. Soon, Chris realized, he would either be blown to pieces at the take-off or he would be speeding along on his hazardous journey.

The great day dawned. Squadron Leader Lambert had insisted that Christopher should take a mild sedative the night before, so he had slept like a top. But he was up early. Fear and excitement chased each other through his thoughts. He found old Whiskers a tower of strength in these last critical moments. "After all," he kept telling himself, "it's what I've wanted, hoped for, prayed for. Why am I having these queasy feelings in my stomach? I'm not afraid; at least I don't think I am."

"Zero minus three hours."

The count-down had begun more than twenty-four hours before the firing. Each stage of the long and complicated drill of testing and fueling the giant rocket had been worked out with Sir Leo Frayling's usual precision. The whole operation, from the start of the count-down to Chris's landing back on the Earth's surface, had been timed to a second, and the chief scientist had before him the master operations sheet which he compared constantly with the continuous flow of reports coming in.

All night long the whole firing area had been brilliantly illuminated while scores of men—British, American, French, and German—worked as a team to prepare Columbus.

Sir George Benson made a brief call to the Gillanders' home while Chris was having breakfast. He was able to report that so far no hitches had occurred, and that the launching was expected to take place exactly on schedule. Chris was to be at the control room not later than 10:30 A.M.

When Sir George had gone, Chris felt the tension within him slowly mounting. Mrs. Gillanders, Betty, Morrey, and the Wing Commander tried hard to keep up a stream of lighthearted conversation, but always Chris's thoughts came back to the adventure before him. His replies became more disjointed and absent-minded as the minutes ticked steadily by. Suddenly he had a thought which, very diffidently, he mentioned to Greatrex. The officer looked at him intently, nodded, and went off in the direction of the control room. It was almost ten o'clock when he returned and informed Chris that all arrangements had been made.

"Of course Frayling went off the deep end," he said, grinning, as he reported on his mission, "but when I said, 'No little service, no pilot for Columbus,' he gave in, with very bad grace. He thought it would dislocate his schedule, but Benson adjusted that in no time. Still, if you're ready, I think we might as well go along now. The padre will join us at control."

Chris stood up with relief, for the minutes had become very heavy. So this was the parting. No one would know what effort went into those bright smiles, those cheerful *au revoirs*, those hearty promises of the good things they would do together after Chris's return. Mrs. Gillanders gave him a quick kiss, shyly followed by Betty. Chris flushed scarlet, much to his own disgust. Morrey shook hands firmly, and Chris wondered just what thoughts were going through his American friend's mind at that moment.

"Come on. You can't stay here all day," said Whiskers. "You've a rocket to catch!"

Abruptly Chris turned and ran out of the bungalow to the waiting jeep. As they sped away toward the firing area he found it impossible to turn his head and wave a final good-bye.

The control room was charged with suppressed excitement. The scientists and engineers were at their posts, checking the multitude of instruments and apparatus which seemed to fill the room. Innumerable telephones were about, and Chris noticed that a call was signaled by a flashing light rather than a ringing bell. In fact he became aware that, in spite of the great activity, the building was as quiet as a church. Everyone seemed to be speaking in whispers except one man who was wearing a telephone operator's headpiece. With monotonous regularity he announced in a loud clear voice the passing of time.

"Zero minus seventy-five minutes."

In a separate room was one vast instrument. This was the computer. Some half-dozen mathematicians gave it their reverent attention, for here would be made the vital calculations affecting all stages of the operation. Should Columbus for any reason deviate from its flight path, Chris knew that in seconds the computer would have worked out the complicated problem of what correction was required. On his return flight the computer would decide the moment of take-off, the angle of ascent, and the duration of thrust.

As the two friends stood a little uncertainly in the center of the control room, Benson and Frayling broke away from what they were doing and came up to them.

"This is most annoying and unnecessary," Sir Leo snapped as he joined them. Chris felt his face beginning to flush, but a wink from Uncle George from behind the chief scientist's back restored the young man's temper. He made no reply to the remark.

"Come into this room," Frayling ordered curtly. "The padre is there already."

Chris, Sir George, and Whiskers followed him silently. True enough, the padre, whom Chris had met several times, was there in his surplice and cassock. He had prepared a small improvised altar and was ready to begin.

"Ten minutes only," the chief scientist snapped as he left them.

With a calm smile the padre beckoned the others to kneel and the short communion service began.

In no more than the time so grudgingly allowed by Sir Leo, it was over, and the three friends quietly thanked the padre and went back into the control room. Chris felt completely calm now. Both Benson and the Wing Commander were delighted at his serenity.

"Zero minus sixty minutes."

For the next fifteen minutes Christopher was questioned by several scientists to make sure that he remembered and fully understood all his instructions. He satisfied them easily, and soon they each shook his hand and wished him luck.

"Now for the suit," Sir George murmured, and led Chris to another room where this weird apparatus was standing. With the assistance of several technicians he put on—or rather climbed into—the heavy suit, and was sealed inside. A deep silence settled on him as all sound from the outside world was completely cut off. In a few seconds the little radio in his helmet crackled and he heard the voice of Sir George, whom he could see talking into a microphone.

"Getting me all right, Chris?" the scientist asked. The young man, with difficulty, raised one of his arms as a signal that all was well.

"Right. Now raise your helmet."

After fumbling for a minute or so Chris was able to swivel back the front of his headgear and breathe the air outside. Around him stood a little knot of men who were watching him anxiously.

"Everything seems all right," he said.

"Good. Then we'd better be off to Columbus," Sir George said with slightly forced cheerfulness.

To save him the effort of walking, a special trolley was brought up and Chris stepped onto it.

"I feel like a piece of luggage," he confessed with embarrassment as he was wheeled out of the building toward the tall, shining rocket.

"No trouble is too much," Whiskers said as he walked alongside his young friend.

At the huge towering gantry which surrounded Columbus, a further indignity awaited Chris. Stepping off the trolley, he felt a loop being slung round him. He was hoisted helplessly into the air. In a few seconds willing hands guided him onto the top platform of the gantry, while Sir George and Whiskers were still puffing as they climbed the stairs below. It was a painful journey for Sir George but he had insisted on making it. Although he was constantly improving, he still had to use his "sticks."

"You beat us to it," the Wing Commander called as he climbed the last few steps a little breathlessly.

Chris was released from the sling and turned to face the aperture by which he must enter the rocket. After a final check to see that he could shut and open his helmet, he turned to bid his two friends good-bye. Even the irrepressible Wing Commander was silent as they gazed uncomfortably at each other.

"All the luck in the world, Chris," Benson said as he rested his hand on his young friend's shoulder.

"And all the luck on the moon as well," Whiskers couldn't resist saying as he put a hand on Chris's other shoulder.

Chris smiled his thanks, for he dared not trust himself to speak. To conceal his emotion he closed his helmet, raised an arm in farewell, and turned toward Columbus. Several men stepped forward to assist him through the opening and onto the couch where he would lie during the journey. When he was comfortably settled Chris removed his helmet, which was not needed inside the cabin.

Instead, once the period of acceleration was over, Chris knew that an anesthetic gas would be introduced automatically into the atmosphere. This would send him into a deep sleep which would last until the rocket began to decelerate for the lunar landing. Experience had shown that this anesthesia not only helped him to overcome the claustrophobia of the small cabin and the boredom of more than two days of inactivity, but it also considerably reduced his consumption of precious oxygen and eliminated his need for food.

In years to come, Chris had heard, astronauts would undergo deep freezing and would stay in a state of suspended animation for weeks, perhaps years. Of course it would require someone to thaw them out at the end of the journey! Meanwhile, he had no worries about his own period of insensibility. He knew that when oxygen was circulated in the cabin again he would wake up none the worse for this blank in his life. He fastened the simple clips of the straps which would hold him down.

"Zero minus five minutes," someone called through the opening.

Now it was time for the aperture to be closed. Chris glanced up to get the last look he would have at daylight on Earth until his task was over. At the opening, briefly, Sir George Benson's face appeared, and for a second the youth and the scientist looked at each other. Then the rectangle was gone; the outside world was shut out; he was on his own.

The radio in the cabin crackled.

"Zero minus four minutes," called the voice of control.

In spite of his determination to remain calm, Chris knew that his heart was beating rapidly. He was sure it was not fear he felt but elation. What matter if he were not so lucky this time? It was what he had wanted, to make his life complete. And if he did—well—get his ticket, what was his life measured against the background of the immeasurable universe? In a few moments he would be leaving the bonds of Earth, a vital part in this wonderful operation that sprang from the finest brains and engineering skill of the whole Western world.

"Zero minus three minutes."

His thoughts were flying on so rapidly that time, too, seemed to have taken wings. All I hope, Chris thought, is that if anything goes wrong, it isn't until after I've set foot on the moon. In a few years' time it will probably be a commonplace experience, but now it will be unique. What would conditions be like on the lunar surface? In his briefings many scientists had done their best to prepare him with information based on the moon satellites and Lunik probes that had been put into orbit. Then there was—

"Zero minus two minutes."

There was his own close look only a year before. But no one was sure, absolutely sure, of what things would actually be like on the moon. If he could land and radio his report back to control, those who came after him would have that knowledge to start with. He would be a true pioneer, blazing the trail for others to follow. He would be making a contribution to the sum total of man's knowledge.

"Zero minus sixty seconds."

It wouldn't be long now. He must relax—relax completely. "Shut your eyes. Breathe deeply," he told himself.

"Ten, nine, eight, seven, six." The calm voice in control called out the fleeting seconds.

"Three, two, one, zero, one, two—"

He was not alarmed at the slight delay. After Columbus had been ignited it would be another few seconds before the power of the thrust from its combustion chamber was sufficient to lift its many tons of weight. Then gently, so gently that he couldn't tell just when it started, Chris felt the rocket move.

"Fifteen, sixteen, seventeen."

Now he could feel himself pushed onto the couch as the rocket picked up speed. Harder and harder he was pressed down by the terrific acceleration, until it was becoming painful. His other rocket flights and his many trips on the centrifuge had prepared him well for the uncomfortable time that lay ahead. As Columbus became ever lighter because of the rapid consumption of its fuel, so the acceleration increased. It was greater than anything he'd had before. It was becoming unbearable. He—couldn't—stand—

Oblivion came to Chris as the giant rocket raced out into empty space.

CHAPTER 8

Not until twelve minutes had passed after the firing switch was pressed did the scientists in control know for sure that the multi-stage rocket had functioned as planned. Now, with the projectile streaking on at over six miles every second, Frayling and his colleagues could tell that Columbus was behaving perfectly. The three spent stages had burned out and been jettisoned; the rocket would now cruise along its predicted path at an ever-decreasing speed.

Long before Earth's gravity had brought it to a standstill it would have come under the moon's influence. With its velocity mounting once more, Columbus would be heading straight for the irregular surface of Earth's satellite. Then the delicate operation of setting the vehicle down would begin. In its final stages Chris would be brought back to consciousness and he would complete the ultimate maneuver.

All the control-room staff, with the exception of Sir Leo Frayling, showed the jubilation they felt at the successful launching of the rocket. The important first stage of Operation Columbus had been completed, and the radio signals from its transmitters were coming in loud and clear. All around the Earth, stations would be receiving the coded messages from the mass of instruments reporting on the projectile's flight.

Already it was out of range of the Australian stations, but stations in Central America were taking over the task. Soon Columbus would be over the Atlantic, and the famous radio telescope at Jodrell Bank in Britain would track its flight. The staff operating the giant spider's web—for so this great instrument appeared—was swinging its huge bowl into position, when one of them noticed an unexpected radar echo on one of the screens in the instrument room. He called the attention of the telescope's director to it at once.

It was not possible to set the big instrument on this mysterious signal, for its task was already decided by international agreement. Instead, a smaller auxiliary instrument was directed to keep track of this unexpected echo. By the time Columbus's signals were coming through, the director was able to announce that the Russians had launched a moon rocket too.

Excitement at Jodrell Bank was intense. The information was flashed to Woomera, which, in turn, requested selected tracking stations to follow the Soviet projectile. At about this time Moscow radio—usually rather reticent about rocket launchings until their success was beyond doubt—announced to the world that Soviet Russia had launched the first man-carrying rocket to the moon. Constantly, repeatedly, all Eastern radio stations broadcast the Moscow announcement, followed by patriotic music and speeches by national leaders. There was much exulting in this Communist achievement which would, for the first time, carry the enlightened doctrine of Karl Marx beyond the confines of Earth.

For the first time since Operation Columbus had begun, the scientists at Woomera saw Sir Leo Frayling's calm broken. When he received the news of the Russian launching, about an hour after the departure of Columbus, his face flushed. The pursed lips, the heavy frown, the rapid breathing were unusual signs of emotions in this unemotional man. Benson and Gillanders waited for the storm to break. With an effort the chief scientist pulled himself together until he was master of his feelings once more.

"You will keep me informed of the progress of both rockets," he snapped to Sir George. "Get the computer at work on the Russian trajectory."

"That will upset the program," Benson pointed out. "We need its full services to compute the flight path of Columbus."

"Nevertheless, you will divert it sufficiently to keep me accurately informed of the Russian progress," Frayling insisted.

Sir George and his deputy protested strongly.

"You know full well how important it is we know exactly how Columbus is functioning," Benson said bitterly. "The safety of young Christopher is at stake."

"May I remind you that he volunteered for this mission," Sir Leo sneered. "He must accept whatever risks there are."

"Then Heaven help you if this causes him any mishap," Billy Gillanders burst out in white-hot fury.

Sir Leo pointedly turned to the latest report that had just been handed to him.

Gradually consciousness returned to Chris as he sped farther and farther from Earth. As his brain began to function again he gazed about him curiously. The intolerable strain caused by the thrust of the giant rocket was gone. Now, he decided, all three stages must have finished their job and he was coasting effortlessly to the moon. Small, soft articles, purposely placed in the cabin, were floating about in the familiar state of free fall. Chris knew that but for the straps which held him to the contour couch he, too, would be bumping weightlessly about his confined quarters.

First he must report to control.

"Hello, control. Hello, control. Columbus reporting to control. Have had blackout but am now fully recovered. Everything seems normal here. Waiting your instructions. Over."

"Hello, Columbus," Sir George's voice came through. "Are you all right, Chris? All stages have functioned perfectly. You're exactly on predicted path. Stand by. Frayling wants to speak to you. Stand by."

Strange, thought Chris. I wonder what he wants? This isn't in the schedule. Something must have happened to make him butt in.

"Hello, Columbus."

It was Sir Leo's voice, all right. Chris listened curiously.

"Hello, Columbus. We have just learned that the Soviet Union launched a manned moon rocket at about the same time as Columbus. The flight path appears to be close to yours. We are delaying your anesthesia. You are to switch on your radar scanner and report any echo."

So that was it! Russia was racing them to it. And he was to watch out for his rival!

"Message received and understood," Chris called back over the radio. Then he reached above his head and flicked over the switch of the radar set.

There was nothing—at least he thought there was nothing. Columbus was spinning slowly, however, and he'd have to wait a bit before he could be certain. No, there was no mysterious blob on his screen. He reported all clear back to control.

"You must keep constant watch and report back at once if you get a reflection," Frayling's crisp order came.

Well, it would give him something to do, Chris thought. According to the original program the anesthetic should now be pumped into his cabin and he would sleep for a couple of days, until he was near the moon. Instead, he was now to keep a lookout for his traveling companion in space and report to Woomera if he spotted him. Obviously he would use more oxygen than if he were unconscious, Chris reflected. "Hope I don't use up too much!" he muttered. Still, Uncle George would have seen to it that he had a fairly wide safety margin. Now where was that Russian chap?

Not for years had the whole world been so electrified. First came the bombastic Soviet broadcasts about its rocket Lenin; then an hour or so later the Western announcement about Operation Columbus. Radio and television programs all round the globe were interrupted to report this fantastic race. Newspapers rushed out special editions. There were official statements from many governments.

Gradually, as more details were filled in about the Eastern and Western projects, it was realized that since both rockets had taken off within a short time of each other, with roughly equal velocities, they must be relatively close to one another. The race to the moon was neck and neck.

People everywhere could talk of nothing else. In buses, offices, factories, on the street, rumor was rife and speculation ran wild. Official broadcasts appealed for calm. The fullest possible information was promised in order to prevent the spread of false information, either by accident or by design of enemy agents.

Soon papers everywhere carried descriptions and photographs of Christopher Godfrey and Serge Smyslov, who were racing it out somewhere in space. There were full accounts of Chris's previous exploits. Both Western and Eastern camps expressed complete confidence in their emissaries to carry out the tasks assigned to them. London, Washington, Paris, and Bonn were sure that Columbus was a better rocket than Lenin. Moscow and Peking hinted darkly that this could only be decided after the safe return of their respective pilots. So all the world was watching what was surely the most fantastic contest since time began— Columbus versus Lenin!

Like Chris, Serge Smyslov recovered consciousness soon after Lenin entered free fall. He was roused by the imperious call of his radio, which seemed to be issuing urgent orders to him. At last he was sufficiently collected to understand the loudspeaker's message. It informed him that the imperialists had launched a moon rocket in an endeavor to rob the Soviet Union of first claim to the moon.

He must report at once if he detected any sign of this Western intruder. His radar must continually scan the surrounding space for its presence. Serge was staggered at the news. He was filled with anger that the capitalists were trying to forestall him and to seize Earth's satellite for their own evil designs. No doubt Moscow would know what to do and would instruct him accordingly.

The young Russian took some little time to become accustomed to his strange condition. Sealed inside the tracked vehicle in which he would make his lunar exploration, Serge's radar was linked to the outer casing of the rocket by a magnetic contact. He switched on the apparatus and peered grimly at the screen.

"They must be less than a thousand miles apart," Sir George Benson stated as he studied reports from the tracking stations. Each rocket was constantly transmitting signals on its own particular wave length. Now more than twenty thousand miles from Earth, the directions from which their signals were coming were almost indistinguishable. It also seemed as if the two projectiles were gradually converging, with Columbus slightly ahead of Lenin.

As the Earth rotated far below the fleeing rockets, station after station sought with eager antennae the stream of radio signals. In the scientific centers of East and West excited men interpreted the data. The results of each calculation were flashed to the government of the nations concerned. Congress, Parliament, Chamber, and *Bundesregierung* were interrupted to give members the latest progress of the two contestants.

To Sir George Benson, Billy Gillanders, and their colleagues in the Woomera control, it seemed that their chief was taking the Russian effort as a personal insult. Sir Leo Frayling followed the progress of the Soviet projectile feverishly. His curt orders to the scientists were, if possible, more peremptory than ever. Only their own overwhelming interest in the progress of events stopped more than one of them from expressing angry resentment. For hour after hour the chief scientist brooded over the successive reports. At intervals he snapped questions over the radio to Chris, who had failed to get a trace of the other rocket on his screen.

Then came a time when young Godfrey hesitated before replying to Frayling's querulous message. The atmosphere in control became one of tense expectancy.

"I think I'm getting something now," came the slightly distorted voice from the loudspeaker.

A torrent of questions poured from the chief scientist. Chris struggled hard to answer them. There was now no doubt about it. Columbus's radar had definitely picked up its fellow traveler. Its range, position, and speed could be worked out from the careful readings Chris made and repeated into his microphone. In control, there was feverish activity around the computer, which was working from the data supplied. In a very short time the answer was given. The Soviet rocket was now some seven hundred and fifty miles from Columbus. It was two hundred miles nearer to Earth, and the flight paths of the two rockets were gradually converging.

"It's too early yet to guess just where they intend to put their rocket down," the astronomers on Sir Leo's staff decided. A great deal depended on the final orbit of the vehicle round the moon, and this was not easy to predict from present information. They would use the past experience which the Americans had in placing a lunar satellite into orbit to make an early assessment of Lenin's possible destination.

Far away in the Western rocket, Chris was still busy with radar observations. The continually interesting task occupied his mind so that he had no feeling of claustrophobia—one of the main reasons for the decision to anesthetize him. The hours slipped by unnoticed. What a pity, he thought, that he had no direct vision of the universe around him. Since it had been anticipated that he would be unconscious for almost the whole of the journey, no provision had been made for him to scan the heavens, except by radar. What was it like, he wondered, in the inky sky around him, with the stars shining with unwinking brightness, the moon above him, and the Earth sinking away far below?

As his eyes turned back to the radar screen the blob of the Russian rocket set his thoughts on another track. Who was inside the Soviet projectile? Who was his unwelcome companion across space? Would they both make a successful landing, and if so, who would be first? What would he do if he met the Russian on the moon? And—just as important—what would the Russian do?

Chris began to feel tired. It was more than eighteen hours since Columbus had been launched and it had been a long period of strain for him. He told control that he thought he should discontinue his observations for a time and try to get some rest. Grudgingly Sir Leo agreed.

"He's using up a good deal of oxygen," Benson said doubtfully. "I suggest we give him the anesthetic for the rest of the journey, as planned."

"Certainly not," the chief scientist snapped. "When

he's had some sleep I want more bearings on this wretched Russian rocket. We'll give him four hours. Then we'll call him over the radio till he wakes again."

"You don't change a bit, Frayling," Benson observed bitterly.

The Russian pilot had detected Columbus just about the same time that his own projectile had been located. He, too, had been ordered to concentrate on tracking the other rocket—the treacherous capitalist space vehicle. Partly by his previous political conditioning, partly by the skillful insinuations he received from some commissar in the Russian control, Serge was stung into a cold fury at the thought of this interloper. Somehow—whether it was subtly suggested to him from the ground or whether it arose from his own thoughts— he knew he must not allow the imperialist emissary to complete his evil mission. If they both made a safe landing and came face to face on the moon, there was no doubt in Smyslov's mind as to what he would do. His eyes fell on the firing trigger of the rocket gun carried by his little tank.

CHAPTER 9

Four hundred miles. Three fifty. Three hundred miles.

The two rockets were now much closer together. As the young pilot of each radioed information back to Earth, their respective control-room staffs debated what action to take.

Sir Leo Frayling, grim and tireless, had scarcely left his post since the launching. Grudgingly he had contacted the different governments participating in Operation Columbus for instructions, and had been given a free hand to take whatever steps were necessary for the successful completion of the operation and the maintenance of Western prestige. Carefully the chief scientist calculated the possibility of expending more of the rocket's precious fuel to ensure that Columbus arrived at the moon first. It was the knowledge that a lunar landing was only half of the job, rather than the angry protests of his colleagues, that persuaded him to abandon the idea.

Benson and the leading scientists of the other national participants in Operation Columbus were of the opinion that events should be allowed to take their course and that they should rely on Godfrey's intelligence and resourcefulness to meet any situation. It was not known, of course, what action, if any, the Russian pilot would be instructed to take. But the unending torrent of bitter abuse from Communist radio stations began to cause serious disquiet to Sir George and his friends.

Professor Boronoff, head of the Russian effort, would have preferred to co-operate with his former colleagues, but he dared not voice this wish to anyone. He was surrounded by Communist Party officials who would have denounced him instantly. There might also, he reflected, be secret agents of the Party among his scientific staff. No, it was too dangerous to express his desire to any other person. He must follow blindly the instructions of a government at the height of an anti-Western campaign. And those instructions were that only the Soviet rocket must return!

The persistent call of his radio roused Christopher Godfrey from the deep sleep into which he had fallen. His first reaction was one of irritation that he had not been allowed to rest. Then, as he became more fully awake, the memory of the Russian rocket flooded back into his mind. He turned to the radar without needing any urging from the loudspeaker.

It was there, all right. The ever-present blip on the screen showed that the race was still on. Carefully Chris transmitted the readings of his instrument to control. Could they tell him, he asked, how near the Soviet rocket was? Did they wish him to remain conscious throughout the journey, or would he be getting the anesthetic for the remainder of the flight? It was half an hour before Frayling's cold voice came back to him.

"The Russian rocket, which they are calling Lenin, is approximately two hundred miles from Columbus. It is on an almost parallel flight path and traveling at the same velocity as yours. What its probable landing area will be we cannot yet say. We are now going to anesthetize you for twenty-four hours. After that you will be restored to consciousness and will so remain for the final twelve hours of your flight. You are to resume reporting radar bearings of Lenin immediately you recover. That is all."

Chris felt a little depressed after the chief scientist had concluded his curt, businesslike message. Not a word of encouragement, not a friendly syllable. Only cold, unemotional orders. Now, thousands of miles from his mother planet, he felt an intense desire to hear a friendly human voice. He must speak to Uncle George, or to Whiskers, or maybe to Billy Gillanders. More than anything else he needed the comfort of a word with his friends.

"May I speak to Sir George?"

He voiced his wish into the microphone a little doubtfully. There was a pause. Then Frayling's voice sounded once more in his ears.

"We are turning on the anesthetic now, Godfrey. You may speak to whomever you please while it is taking effect. I'm putting Benson on to you now."

Chris's heart gave a little skip of joy as the voice of his friend came through.

"Hello, Chris lad. You're still all right, are you? You've done a great job so far. Bit of a licker about the Russian, isn't it? Anyway, I don't suppose you'll see anything of him, even if he does make a successful landing."

"Hello, Uncle George. Yes, I'm fine. Just a bit stiff from being still so long. Will you be there when I make the landing?" Ah! He could hear the slight hissing noise in his cabin as the valve on the anesthetic supply was opened by radio from control.

"Yes, I'll be here all the time. I'm going to get my sleep while you get yours. Everything has worked one hundred per cent perfectly so far," Benson assured him. "We're going to make a great success of Operation Columbus."

"Sure we will. Is—is—Whiskers there?" Chris asked. He knew he was starting to go under. The familiar singing noise had started in his ears and his thoughts were becoming jumbled.

"Hello, young feller-me-lad," came the breezy voice of the Wing Commander. "You're having a great flip so far. Don't worry a bit about that Communist bloke. He won't bother you. Have a good sleep. We'll be here when you wake. Now here's Billy to have a word with you."

"Hello, Chris. Are you still awake?" Gillanders asked. "Can you hear me, Chris?"

There was no reply. Chris had sunk into the deep sleep of anesthesia from which he would not recover until nearing the moon.

Inside the other fleeting speck crossing the black emptiness of space, the young Communist stuck grimly to his task. Not for him the gentle release of unconsciousness, but rather the wakefulness caused by the drug amphetamine which he was ordered to take from time to time. Constantly he called out the bearings of Columbus, which now seemed very near, compared with the vast distance which separated the two rockets from any other body.

Occasionally it was Boronoff's voice which came to him over the ether, but usually it was that of some Party official adding another little drop of poison. What right, Serge asked himself, had the West to intrude in this great Soviet adventure? Here was proof, if proof were needed, of the capitalists' constant attempts to frustrate Russia's great plans. Here was proof that they feared the Soviet's great scientific achievements and were forever straining to imitate them.

At some time—he hardly knew when—it was borne in on the young Russian's mind that his primary task was no longer the exploration of the moon and an attempt to discover the nature and origin of the mysterious domes of Pico. Rather, it was to destroy the enemy, or at least to prevent his rival from ever returning home to Earth.

Sir Leo Frayling had accepted the perfect performance of the rocket Columbus without comment. In this gigantic piece of engineering there were over half a million different component parts, with many thousands of them quite capable of ruining the whole project if they failed to function correctly. So many things could go wrong with what was perhaps the most complicated piece of mechanism ever made by man! But nothing had gone wrong—so far.

Memories were still vivid of the intense disappointments of the earlier days, when it was a chancy business whether a rocket even took off or not. It was that early rocket work, however, which had enabled vehicles like Columbus to be made almost completely reliable. Yet there was quiet jubilation among the scientists at Woomera and among their fellows in the Western countries that Columbus was functioning so perfectly. The rocket was approaching the moon exactly as predicted.

At a signal from Sir Leo Frayling, Squadron Leader Lambert sent out the impulse which would start changing the atmosphere in the projectile's cabin. The anesthetic would be shut off and the supply of oxygen would be increased. As Chris gradually came back to consciousness this would be recorded on a small collection of instruments which indicated his pulse and respiration. They showed the stronger heart beat and deeper breathing as Chris responded to the changed atmosphere. Soon he should be reporting over the radio.

Sir George and young Godfrey's other friends in control listened anxiously for the first sounds from the loudspeaker. When they came they were unintelligible, for Chris was still struggling back from his long sleep. At last they heard the expected message.

"Hello, control. I'm all right again now. Awaiting your instructions."

"Sure you're all right, Chris?" At a sign from the chief scientist, Benson had taken over the microphone. "Well, before you do anything else, have some glucose and a few meat tablets. We want you a hundred per cent fit, you know."

Obediently the young man reached up and unclipped a tube, shaped like a very large toothpaste tube, from the side of the cabin. He unscrewed the top, placed the end to his mouth, and squeezed out a few drops of the refreshing fluid. To drink out of a cup would have been impossible in the rocket's weightless condition. Any liquid would have escaped and broken up into tiny fugitive droplets. Before replacing the cap Chris could not resist the temptation to squeeze out a few more drops. The little shining spheres floating about never ceased to fascinate him. Then, slowly, he chewed a couple of meat tablets—those unexciting but nourishing preparations on which he would have to exist until his return to Earth.

"Now, Chris, let's have the latest position of Lenin," Uncle George requested.

From the observations the young man transmitted, Benson was able to inform him a few minutes later that the two rockets were now a mere forty miles apart. Unless the Russians put their projectile into some unexpected orbit, it seemed that Chris and the Russian pilot would become comparatively near neighbors on the moon. What neither the Western scientists nor their Russian counterparts yet realized was that both had chosen the relatively flat surface inside the crater Plato for the first lunar landing.

Christopher was now becoming quite excited. Before many more hours the landing maneuver would commence. Though he had been near to the satellite before, and though a number of successful lunar probes had revealed many of its secrets, conditions on the moon's surface remained a mystery. Was it actually covered with a layer of dust, as many astronomers supposed? If so, how thick was the layer? Would he find any of the surface flat and smooth, or would every square yard be pitted with craterlets too small to have been seen by the best telescopes or by the television cameras in lunar satellites?

Suppose, after all, Plato was not flat. How would it affect his landing? Would he see anything of the mysterious silver streaks that crossed mountain and valley in fairly straight lines for hundreds of miles? And finally, but most breathtaking of all, would he encounter the builders of those frightening artificial structures, the domes of Pico?

There were many jobs for Chris to do. From now on he must turn his attention solely to the moon. For some time Columbus had been under the influence of its pull and the rocket was building up a considerable velocity under the influence of lunar gravity. Accurate readings of his distance from the surface were of vital importance. He must also identify as soon as possible the area toward which the rocket was speeding. From this information control would be able to work out the operation that would turn Columbus into an orbit that should carry it over Plato.

The flick of another switch brought upon the television screen a blurred and moving image which Chris knew to be the moon. Adjusting some of the controls, he was able to sharpen the picture, but he was still too many thousands of miles away to recognize any particular feature. He had become very familiar with the moon's geography from long hours of studying lunar photographs. He had no doubt that when he came a little closer he would be able to pinpoint his position. He glued his eyes to the screen before him.

"He's certainly used more oxygen than we'd allowed for," one of the scientists was reporting to Billy Gillanders. "That long spell of consciousness and the activity of reporting the position of the Russian rocket were never foreseen. I'd say he'll have to cut down his stay on the moon by about six hours."

"Thanks, Jim. I'll let Sir George and Frayling know." There was a little frown of worry on the big Australian's forehead as he walked across to where the Columbus director and Sir George were standing.

"The oxygen consumption has been above schedule," Billy reported. "We shall have to modify the lunar exploration."

"I expected that," Benson answered seriously. "How much shall we have to cut out?"

"I shall decide if any alterations will be made to the program," the chief scientist interrupted coldly. "Please concern yourself with preparations for the landing maneuver."

"Then don't leave the modifications till it's too late," Sir George said grimly. He turned and hobbled away with Billy to join Dr. Rosenberg and a small group of top scientists.

"Trouble with the old boy?" the American inquired, seeing the set faces of his friends.

"He's inhuman!" Billy burst out. "He's nothing but a scientific machine." He told the others about the oxygen, and how Benson and he had been snubbed.

"Don't worry. If necessary we'll all have something to say about that," Rosenberg promised.

"Ptolemaeus!" Chris exclaimed excitedly. "I'm sure that's Ptolemaeus. Yes, and there's Alphons and Arzachel!"

He continued to call out the names of the great lunar craters as he recognized them on his screen. The rocket was now so much nearer the moon that he had no difficulty in picking out the familiar features, which seemed like old friends. There was the Mare Nubium, and at the edge of his screen he could see the mysterious light-colored rays that he knew spread out in all directions from the great crater of Tycho. Unfortunately the areas in which he was most interested—around the strange little mountain called Pico and the crater Plato—were off his screen. Still, he had identified his position. It seemed from his screen that he was heading straight for the center of the satellite.

His messages were acknowledged by control. Chris knew that on Earth they were making the final calculations to turn Columbus into an orbit that would carry him toward his destination.

"We shall be starting the motor in seventeen minutes' time," the voice of Sir Leo came up to him. "You know precisely what you have to do when you are in orbit?"

Of course he knew. Hadn't he gone over the whole drill a hundred times? His job was to plot exactly his new course. The lunar landscape would be moving across his screen and he must follow the course of Columbus. Then he would have to fire the small auxiliary rocket engines placed at each side of the main motor, which would cause the projectile to veer either to the right or to the left as required. By this means he would guide the rocket until it headed straight toward the landing area. He'd have to be pretty sharp with his readings then, for if the retro-rockets were fired at the wrong time he would either crash onto the moon or miss his target altogether.

As the minutes ticked by, Chris looked at the craters on his screen. He remembered the terrific interest aroused some years before when a Russian astronomer announced that he had observed an active volcano on one side of the central peak of the crater Alphons. Although spectroscopic analysis of the light reflected from this area revealed an unaccountable excess of carbon—a fairly certain sign of volcanic activity—there had never been any definite confirmation of the Russian's claim. The resulting controversy had divided astronomers ever since. How he longed to be able to settle the argument one way or another! Yet that was not his task.

A quivering began to shake the cabin. The loose articles which had been floating around him during his free flight had now all settled on one side. The landscape began to move across the television screen. New craters and mountain ranges were coming into view. It was fascinating to call out the names of each of the features as he recognized them. Control acknowledged his reports and plotted the new course for Columbus. Now the rocket was moving almost parallel to the rough lunar surface. Chris wondered which of the small auxiliary rockets he would have to fire.

Keenly he watched the shifting scene. That towering range of mountains was the Apennines; its fearsome peaks seemed to point angrily at the unwelcome visitor. Ah! That was the famous crater Archimedes with its seemingly smooth surface. From Earth the floor of this circular plain, more than fifty miles in diameter, appeared flat and without the usual central peak or numerous small craters. But Chris could see now that it was pockmarked with tiny depressions in the familiar chain pattern. The walls surrounding Archimedes were relatively low—about four thousand feet high, he guessed.

From the direction Columbus was traveling, Chris decided that its course would have to be turned a few degrees to his left to bring him over the notorious Pico area. There he would see for the first time at close quarters the frightening devastations made by the atomic missiles launched from Earth. Then he would pass over toward the crater Plato which had been chosen as his landing point. And then the delicate and dangerous operation of putting Columbus down onto the lunar surface would begin.

A one-and-a-half seconds' burst on one of the auxiliary rockets would be sufficient, control decided. If he would preset his timing instrument it would tell him when to fire. Chris reached up and twisted a pointer on the seconds dial to one point five, and awaited developments.

"Fire the rocket ten seconds from now," came the disembodied voice, which then went on with the countdown.

At the correct instant Chris pressed the firing switch. Almost instantly he felt the response of Columbus. The click of the timing apparatus told him that the short burst had been completed, so he peered eagerly at his screen to observe the new course. Directly in front of him was a lonely mountain peak, pointing upward like an accusing finger. It stood out from the pitted lunar plain in comparative isolation. For a moment Chris's heart stood still. For a split second he thought he had recognized the famous mountain Pico, neighbor to the sinister domes he had helped to destroy.

It wasn't Pico. A second later he realized that the object of his scrutiny was its near twin, Piton. Yes, that little craterlet in the summit was positive identification. Besides, there was no evidence of the devastation he expected to find near the real target.

Was he now on the right course? Control would soon let him know if any further action was required. This would have to be taken quickly if he was not to miss the landing area altogether. Already Piton was slipping off his screen, so he must be very near to the critical area.

Ah! That small bright crater must be Piazzi Smyth. Then Columbus must be heading straight for the radioactive desert around Pico. Chris's pulse began to race with excitement as he described his course to the distant listeners. He tried to adopt the technique of radio commentators and to give a word picture of the scene before him.

"Confine yourself to accurate observation," Frayling's voice came back like a cold shower. Chris felt a momentary wave of anger, but he continued his description in a precise, unemotional manner worthy of the chief scientist himself.

Suddenly his new-found calm was shattered. On his screen had appeared a scene like nothing he had seen before. Hills had been leveled, craters obliterated, ridges and rays completely wiped away. The whole area, taking up ever more of his field of view, seemed as if it had been fused in a vast furnace. Whether it was reflected light from the glossy surface, or whether it was glowing of its own accord, Chris could not tell; but all the region seemed unnaturally bright compared with the rest of the moon.

A flashing light warned him that Columbus was passing over an area of intense radioactivity. Then this must be the place where the alien domes had been blasted away! This place had been the target of the atomic rockets sent to destroy the source of harmful radiation bombarding the earth. It must have been somewhere here that he had placed down the Levy beacon enabling the deadly missiles to complete their task. But where was Pico? Had that eight-thousand-foot mountain been blasted away too? Surely that little hillock—barely a few hundred feet high—was not all that remained of the well-known peak?

While he was absorbed in watching this fearsome scene, Chris suddenly felt a shudder pass through the rocket. He had a momentary feeling of alarm. Had the radioactivity of this blighted area affected Columbus in some way? Were the beings who had built the domes still on the moon and were they trying to wreak vengeance on this Earthly intruder? Then the real reason for the sensation dawned upon him. It was caused by the firing of retro-rockets in the forefront of his vehicle. Control had performed the operation by an electrical impulse. The landing maneuver had begun!

CHAPTER 10

Christopher's pulse increased greatly with the terrific excitement he felt. The last vital part of his outward journey had begun—the dangerous and highly complicated operation of slowing Columbus down and then landing it gently within the crater Plato. Soon—within minutes, perhaps—the rocket would crash into the lunar rocks, or it would settle quietly down and he would be able to step out into the fantastic new world around. So he would be the first human to set foot on another world—or would he?

For some time Chris had forgotten about his Russian rival. Preoccupied with his duties and with observing the strange new scene, Chris had not given the Russian rocket a thought. Now it had come to his mind and he wondered desperately what had happened to the young Communist. Had he already landed and so robbed the Columbus pilot of the honor of being first?

The stern voice of Sir Leo recalled Chris to his tasks. Now, more than ever, accurate observation of the rocket's position was important. He must act in split seconds to adjust the projectile's course if necessary. Already the retro-rockets had succeeded in slowing Columbus considerably; it must now be sinking down toward Earth's satellite. When it was over Plato, a final burst from the retro-rocket would remove all forward motion and the vehicle would commence its fall toward the lunar surface.

Plato! Moving slowly, the great circular feature now came on the screen. Chris knew that this famous crater, eighty miles in diameter and with rocky walls four thousand feet high, was thought to be the flattest part of the moon's surface. Yet even this was not sure, for often observers had seen mysterious changes on its floor.

It was generally agreed that Plato was one of those places on the moon where a strange mist could sometimes be seen creeping across the ground. At times small marks could be seen within its walls, while at other times those same marks were invisible. It looked to Chris darker than the rest of the moon, as it seemed to settle almost exactly in the center of the screen.

Now must come perhaps the most delicate part of the landing operation. The base of the rocket must be turned toward the lunar surface. Then, by igniting the main motor again, the vehicle's fall would be decelerated. Because of there being no appreciable atmosphere around the moon, there would be no atmospheric braking to help the rocket fall with the heavier base first.

The whole vehicle would have to be turned by means of the small auxiliary rockets, and therein lay the difficulty. Once the projectile was made to turn, it would continue to twist over and over, since there was no aerodynamic control in the vacuum of space. To overcome this an ingenious gyroscope mechanism had been installed which would automatically fire an opposing rocket sufficient to correct the turning motion. Other small rockets at different points around Columbus's casing would be brought into play by the gyroscope if necessary. Once the base was pointing squarely at the lunar surface, it would be kept there during the rest of the descent.

As he reported the position of Plato on his screen, Chris felt the rocket begin to turn. Immediately the great crater swam out of his view and he had to switch to a second screen, which revealed the scene directly astern. For a few seconds mountains and craters rushed madly about the second screen, moving first one way, then the other. Then everything settled down—and there was good old Plato slap in the center. Chris heaved a sigh of relief. Another obstacle was overcome, and now he was rushing at ever-increasing speed toward the strange terrain below.

"Two hundred and forty-six thousand feet," he called into the microphone as he noted from instruments the rocket's height above the moon.

Hardly had he spoken when Chris felt himself crushed heavily into his contour couch. The motor had been ignited by control and the slowing-down process had begun. Sensations similar to those he had felt when Columbus was launched confused him for a moment. It was hard to realize that the projectile was losing rather than gaining speed. He felt that he was being forced away from the moon, just as he had been lifted fiercely from Earth two days before.

"Two—hundred—thousand."

It was all that Christopher could do to gasp out the altitude reading. The pressure upon him was so great that he could scarcely move his facial muscles.

Plato loomed much larger now. It filled all the screen, and as he watched the mountainous rim passed slowly out of the picture. But his physical discomfort was so great that Chris found it almost impossible to observe the lunar scene closely.

"One—hundred—fifty," he forced himself to call.

Not until Columbus was less than fifty thousand feet above the crater floor did the pressure slacken.

Against the comparatively weak gravity of the satellite the powerful thrust of the motor had decelerated the rocket rapidly. Now the combustion of the engine had been reduced to a minimum and the surface was rising up to meet the rocket at a mere two hundred miles an hour.

Eagerly now Chris peered at the new world that was awaiting him. While much of the area toward which Columbus was speeding seemed flat enough, there were parts which abounded with craterlets which reminded him of pockmarks after smallpox. Faint marks wavered about at random. In a few places they were thicker and heavier—crevasses, most likely, he thought.

For a time Chris forgot to call out the altitude. A sharp reminder from Frayling recalled him with a jerk.

"Thirty thousand. Twenty-nine. Twenty-eight."

It wouldn't be long now! Chris was tense with excitement. He was no higher than Everest from the landing point, and the mountains surrounding the crater had long since moved off his screen. Where exactly would he touch down? Would Columbus remain upright, or would it fall on its side? If it fell over, Chris reflected grimly, that would make the prospects of its take-off back to Earth very questionable.

"Twenty. Nineteen. Eighteen."

Only three and a half miles to go. Another short burst from the motor slowed Columbus still more. Except if an accident happened, it was pretty certain that the landing would be gentle. A stream of instructions now began to come over the radio. Chris was not to attempt to leave the cabin until told to do so, as it would be necessary to make numerous instrumented observations of conditions on the lunar surface before control could be absolutely sure that it was safe for him to proceed outside.

"Not that Sir Leo's worried about my personal safety," the young man muttered to himself. "He's only concerned about the success of the scientific undertaking."

At eight thousand feet Chris pulled the lever which extended the three retractable legs with which the base of the rocket was fitted. These would act as shock absorbers and would help to support the rocket in a vertical position. From the altimeter it was plain that the rate of descent was now very much slower. He was actually inside the crater, with the sheer mountains all around him, somewhere beyond the horizon. Once the rocket motor was fired a little too fiercely and Columbus shot up a few hundred feet before the correction was made. The screen was now useless, for the rocket was too near the ground. Chris now had no way of knowing what was below him.

As he waited, the seconds ticked by. What would the surface be like? he wondered. Somewhere he had read of a theory that the layer of dust which was supposed to cover the ground might be highly dangerous. It might, after countless ages of exposure to unscreened sunlight, be explosive, only waiting for some foreign body to spark off a terrific upheaval. Well, he'd know now in less than a minute, for Columbus was settling down evenly with only a few hundred feet to go.

"All set, Chris?"

This time it was Sir George Benson's voice that sounded in the cabin. Chris brightened at the sound. It was good to know that Uncle George was standing by; it gave him a sense of confidence.

"Yes, all set and ready to go," Chris called back gaily. Then he lay back waiting for the bump. There was nothing else he could do.

It was quite a heavy one. As Columbus hit the surface of Earth's satellite the shock strained every part of the cabin. Chris had a moment of fear. Would the casing be fractured? Had the rocket been badly damaged? Would it be able to take off again? These and a score of other questions troubled him as he collected his wits to face the situation. Well, at least he was alive and was now somewhere on the face of a strange new world.

All was deadly silent until the loudspeaker crackled. Thank God that was working!

"Are you all right, Chris? Have you landed?" came the anxious questions from Benson.

"Yes, I'm fine. Columbus landed rather heavily, though," he called back.

"Good. Now listen carefully. First of all, is there any change in pressure inside the cabin?"

Chris twisted to look at one of the dials.

"No," he answered, "it seems pretty steady."

"Well, watch that carefully for the next hour. If it shows any sign of falling you'll have to try and locate the leak. You've plenty of plastic metal that will do the job, if you can find where to put it. Now what position are you in? Can you release yourself from the couch?"

Chris could just reach one of the several rubber balls that had been put in the cabin for him to observe the different gravity conditions. While in free fall they had floated about, but now they were all in one corner of the cabin floor. He held the ball up and then released it to watch it drop. It seemed to fall quite slowly. This, he knew, was because lunar gravity was only one sixth of Earth's.

"I should say we're leaning about fifteen degrees," he said. "I'm going to get off the couch now."

His gloved fingers were terribly stiff, in spite of regular exercise. He found it a slow job to release himself, even though all fasteners were specially designed. At last he was free. He gingerly flexed his legs. How good it was to be able to move about again! When the circulation was nearly back to normal, Chris swung himself off the couch.

The rocket certainly was leaning, though he could

stand on the floor without difficulty. As he moved he had the strangest sensation—as if he were swimming beneath an invisible sea which supported him but did not impede his movements. Like the ball, he touched the floor very lightly. He described his experience over the radio to Uncle George.

"Any sign of radioactivity?" the scientist asked.

"Only an occasional tick from the counter," Chris told him.

"That's all right. You're bound to get that with no atmosphere. Let me have a count spread over five minutes. Be as accurate as you can."

"Ninety-seven," Chris called back at the end of the period.

"Safe enough," Benson assured him. "Well, I suppose you're anxious to have a look outside. 'Fraid you'll have to wait a bit longer yet. Test your helmet and oxygen cylinders while you're waiting."

"Right," Chris answered cheerfully.

He turned to the wall of the cabin on which ten cylinders were clamped. Each could supply him with sufficient oxygen to last four hours. Forty hours. The time he'd been allowed to wander around the moon to discover as much as possible was thirty hours, to give him a comfortable margin. First, he knew, he was to step out of the rocket and report on conditions outside. Then he would take a longer walk, then one still longer. Finally he would have to get as near to the crater's edge as possible, to try to peer over the rim and see the devastated area outside.

While he was waiting for the minutes to tick by, Chris kept up a cheerful conversation with his friends back on Earth. After Sir George, he talked with Whiskers and Billy Gillanders. All the time he kept his eye anxiously on the pressure gauge, but the needle remained steady. Columbus had stood the shock of landing. Fifteen minutes before he was due to open the hatch and step outside, Frayling took over. The cold, precise voice failed to quell the bubbling excitement the young man felt. He acknowledged his instructions lightheartedly. Then an idea occurred to him.

"Can you tell me, sir," he asked, "if the Russian has landed—and where?"

There was silence for a few moments, then Frayling's voice came back again.

"We have no up-to-date information about the Soviet rocket, but it will undoubtedly have landed by now. We believe it also has landed within Plato. You are to report immediately if you see anything of the rocket or its pilot."

"Very good, sir."

Chris clipped one of the oxygen cylinders onto his back. Each was numbered, and he was to use them in the correct order so that he would always know how many full cylinders were left. He would put on his helmet and change over to the cylinder at the last possible moment. Five minutes before the hour was up, the order came from Sir Leo to exhaust the air from the cabin.

Chris downed his helmet and switched on a motor which would pump out the oxygen in the cabin and store it under pressure in a sealed tank. He knew there were several reasons for this. Owing to restrictions on space, it had been impossible to design a suitable air lock. Also, it would be much easier to open the hatch if the pressure inside and outside were nearly equal.

As he waited for the pump to finish its job, Chris watched his pressure suit inflate. He himself felt no different, though his swollen suit made it a little more difficult to move. At last the pressure in the cabin was as low as it was possible to get it. The great moment had come when he would open the hatch, step through it, and gaze at the world outside.

"Are you ready?" Frayling's voice asked.

Though Chris's heart was beating almost too much for him to reply, he managed to croak an affirmative.

"Right. Then open the hatch and go outside."

"Good luck!" Sir George's voice came through in the background.

Tensing himself, Christopher seized the handle of the catch, twisted it, and swung the door wide open.

As Sir Leo Frayling had surmised, the Soviet rocket Lenin also had landed in Plato. Unlike that of Columbus, its touchdown had been gentle. By sheer good luck the rocket was on level ground and was standing upright.

Serge, like his British counterpart, was bounding with excitement to explore this new world—for the greater glory of the Soviet Union. The crisp, curt commands from the Russian control came through clearly as he prepared the minitank for its excursion outside. Unlike Columbus, the cabin of the Russian rocket did not have to be pumped free of air. Indeed, the tank itself was the actual cabin, and this was sealed to carry its atmosphere with it.

Readings of radioactivity and temperature outside were sent back before Serge received permission to proceed. His final instructions contained a reminder that the imperialists' rocket must be fairly close; he was to proceed with caution until he had located it. The young Russian had his own ideas about what he would do if he saw it, little guessing that they had been deliberately planted within him by his masters.

In grim exaltation he raised one of the pincer-like arms of his tank and released the doorway in the casing. He could hear the hum of his electric motors as he inched ahead. The touch of his vehicle caused the door to fall forward and form a ramp leading down to the surface. With a lurch the minitank moved onto the ramp and then out into the strange world.

CHAPTER 11

Peering through the open hatch, Christopher Godfrey first saw a blinding light. A flick of a finger caused a polarized screen to slip in front of his helmet. He could now take his first real look at the surface of the moon.

In a wide circle around the rocket, bare brown rock shone in the intense rays of the sun. The ground, Chris saw before he stepped through the door, was pitted with small, shallow holes which looked like minute craters. Where was the layer of dust that astronomers had confidently predicted? Certainly there was none around Columbus. Then Chris thought of the reason. The blast from the rocket motor as it neared the moon's surface would scatter anything that was loose. The lack of atmosphere would cause any dust to settle quickly in a new place, leaving the surrounding area clear.

Raising his head, Christopher gazed farther afield. Undulations and more craters seemed to be the general pattern. Some distance away he could see a change in the color of the ground from brown to a bluey-gray.

This, he decided, must be the lunar dust. One of his tasks was to discover as much about it as possible.

The distance from the hatch to ground level was about eight feet. A series of recesses had been made in the rocket casing to help in climbing down. Chris, however, decided that he would make his debut onto the moon in a more spectacular manner than by climbing tamely down the recesses. Pausing for a moment on the rim, he leaped forward from the opening.

On earth a jump from a height of eight feet could cause trouble unless done properly, using the flexed legs as shock absorbers. Chris, fit in every way, was quite used to such exercises and automatically prepared himself for the landing. But instead of falling down alongside Columbus as he had expected, Chris found that his leap had carried him some distance away from the rocket.

His fall to the ground seemed ludicrously slow. He rolled over in surprise as he touched it, then scrambled to his feet and looked around. He knew that the temperature was very high and that only the insulation of his suit prevented him from succumbing to the intense solar heat.

"We're waiting for your report," Frayling's voice sounded in his helmet.

The small receiver-transmitter in the headgear was not strong enough to communicate directly with Earth. Signals to and from it were picked up and relayed on by the more powerful apparatus in Columbus. Fifty miles was the maximum range which Chris could reach and still keep contact through Columbus with control. He spoke back to Sir Leo, carefully describing the scene to him.

Next Chris walked around the rocket to report on its position. This was important so that control would know the hazards of take-off. As he set off to do the job he again experienced the peculiar effect of the low gravity. Each time he lifted his foot to take a step forward his whole body rose a few inches from the ground. Soon he discovered that the most effective form of locomotion was to go forward in leaps like a kangaroo.

He could see now the cause of Columbus's angle. The rocket had touched down on the edge of a small crater about ten feet in diameter, with surrounding walls a couple of feet high. One of the landing legs was planted firmly on top of the wall, making the projectile look very much like a miniature tower of Pisa. There were no other obstructions. It seemed to Chris that Columbus would be able to take off normally, except that control would have to make a correction to its flight path as soon as it was off the ground.

After reporting this, Chris's next job was to collect a sample of the lunar dust. He returned to his cabin for a lead container and a Geiger counter. This time his jump from the hatch was more successful. He set off toward the edge of the area the rocket had blasted clear, making the short distance in four or five leaps.

At the edge he paused and looked at the age-old dust which extended as far as he could see. Bending down, he held the Geiger counter near. Only an occasional flick of the needle was registered. At least, Chris concluded, the dust was not very radioactive. He scooped up some dust and sealed it in the metal container.

It was when he bent closer that Chris noticed a most peculiar thing. Looking intently, it seemed that the blue-gray powder was in motion. Grains of it kept leaping up a little and then falling back as if they were performing a weird native dance. It looked something like a strange boiling pot. Involuntarily Chris drew back his hand, which he had extended to gather up another sample. Then he noticed something else.

As his arm, which cast a shadow far sharper and deeper than an earthly shadow, moved over the surface, the dust in the shade remained still, only to begin its contortions as soon as it came into the sunlight again. He reported the phenomenon to control. Frayling theorized that this peculiar movement was due either to the impact of micro-meteorites—cosmic dust too small to see—or to the intense radiation from the sun. He reminded Chris that here there was no atmosphere to consume the tiny meteors by friction and to form a shield against radiation.

Chris filled the lead container and screwed on the top, then stood up to gaze around. As far as he could see, the lunar dust covered the surface, except where small, sharp pinnacles a few feet high pushed through. Bright sunlight and black shadows were everywhere, for the sun was now at quite an angle to the ground. In the far distance beyond the horizon, Chris knew, were the mountains which formed the rim of the great crater. He could not see anything of them, for they were many miles away. Neither could he see any trace of the Russian rocket. He felt alone, completely alone, in a dead and dusty world.

As if to contradict this feeling, the loudspeaker in Chris's helmet crackled. Sir George's voice came through.

"Now then, Chris, for the next stage," the scientist called out. "We haven't much time to spare, as you know. After you've put the dust sample back in the rocket, hitch up another oxygen cylinder. We want you to move toward the edge of Plato nearest the Pico area. But don't go too far. Keep in sight of Columbus. Take the Geiger with you and collect some rock samples if you can. Don't be more than two hours away. This will give you a chance to practice those leaps of yours! And keep up a running commentary on your journey."

"I'll try," the young man answered gaily, wondering if perhaps the low gravity was having an intoxicating effect.

The minitank lurched down the ramp from the Soviet rocket and onto the rocky ground below. Now the young Communist must perform what some might regard as the most important part of his assignment. Once he was firmly on the moon he stopped the tank. In a clear, ringing voice, which he knew would be carried back to Earth and re-broadcast by all Soviet transmitters, he spoke aloud.

"In the name of the U. S. S. R. and of the Communist Party, I take possession of the moon and declare it to be a Republic in the Soviet Union."

So saying, he released from beneath the vehicle a red metallic star. This was to mark the exact spot on which he had taken formal possession of Earth's satellite, and was so inscribed. Then he moved the tank forward as the cheers of far-distant comrades sounded in his ears.

A great day for the Soviet Union! A great day for him, Serge Smyslov. His name would be recorded in the history books of future generations, along with those of Marx, Lenin, Stalin, and Khrushchev. Nothing, nothing, must be allowed to rob him or his country of this glorious honor!

His next job was to survey the surrounding area and to try to locate the imperialists' rocket—that is, if it had succeeded in making a landing. What would happen then—well, Serge knew quite clearly what he would do. The strange little vehicle moved forward like a great beetle amid the fantastic silent scene. Serge kept his eyes open for any sign of the enemy, meantime collecting dust and rock samples by means of the claw-like arms which made the minitank look more than ever like a huge insect.

Several times Serge returned to the rocket to deposit the samples or to obtain a fresh supply of oxygen. Then he was ordered to rest before making a long journey toward the crater's edge. With a last look around to make sure that there was no sign of the Western intruder, he drove his tank back inside the missile and did as he was instructed.

Chris found it very exhilarating to be able to take these great leaps. He replenished his oxygen supply and set off on his excursion away from Columbus, carrying the Geiger counter. In his childhood he had read in fairy stories of seven-league boots, and he remembered how badly he had wanted a pair. Now he found that with little effort he could sail forward four or five yards at each stride. It was great fun and he covered the ground quickly.

Everywhere the scene was repeated—hillocks, craters of all sizes, and the dancing dust. His direction had been given to him by control, which used the angle of the sun shadows as a guide. He was to travel toward the sun, but at an angle of about fifteen degrees to the right of its line of shadow. This was the direction of the rim nearest the sinister Pico area. A Levy beacon installed in Columbus enabled his radio-compass needle always to show him the way back.

Christopher carefully carried out his instructions. He gave a description—a little gay, when Benson was receiving—of all he could see. Periodically he took a reading from the counter, but there was no appreciable increase in radioactivity. He was now about four miles away from his base, but he could still see the leaning Columbus shining in the distance. Frayling's voice ordered him back to the rocket to prepare for the important journey right to Plato's edge.

When he had climbed inside his cabin and had sealed the hatch, Chris turned the valve that would release oxygen from the tank into which it had been pumped before he went outside. Not until the pressure in the compartment reached a certain figure could he remove his helmet and relax. Although it had been a wonderful experience to move about on the moon, he was glad to stretch out on the couch and rest. He was to remain there for several hours; he must eat, drink, and try to have a short sleep. Control would call him when he was to resume his duties.

Gratefully Chris lay back. He swallowed some food, than chatted with his friends on Earth. First he talked to Uncle George, then to Whiskers, Gillanders, and Dr. Rosenberg. He must have fallen asleep quite soon after this. In his sleep he had a dream. He had flown to the moon in a rocket which had been smashed when he landed, making it impossible for him to return to Earth. All around the wrecked missile the dust seemed to be doing a war dance in glee at the intruder's misfortune. Suddenly in his dream he saw another rocket, tall, shining, with a huge red star painted on its side.

"Can you give me a lift back to Earth?" Chris asked, knocking at the hatch. It was flung open and there appeared the grinning face of a bald-headed man. In one hand he held a glass of vodka. With a sweeping gesture he drained the glass, flung it on the ground outside, and slammed the hatch door. Oh, well, Chris knew it was all a dream, for wasn't he actually in bed in his room at Cambridge?

No, he couldn't be! There was no loudspeaker in his bedroom, no voice telling him he must wake up. With a struggle he forced his eyes to open. Heavens! Where was he? It was just like being in the cabin of a rocket! In a blinding flash, memory came back. So he was on the moon after all! Thank goodness, the part of his dream about Columbus being smashed was not true.

"Are you awake, Godfrey? Are you awake?"

The annoying voice of the chief scientist was sufficient to arouse the young man completely. He reported that he was awake and ready for instructions.

"Your journey must last no longer than twenty-four hours," Sir Leo began. "You have already consumed six hours' supply of oxygen. That leaves enough for the twenty-four-hour journey. We estimate that you are about twenty miles from the rim mountains near the area to be investigated. You report your speed to be some six miles per hour without undue exertion. Therefore the journey there and back will take you about seven of the twenty-four hours. The seventeen hours remaining should be ample for you to scale the mountain, obtain what information you can, and approach Pico until we tell you the radioactivity is dangerous. Have you understood?"

"Perfectly, thank you," Godfrey answered drily.

"Take some food now. You will be unable to eat again until you return to Columbus. Let us know when you are about to evacuate the air from the cabin."

So that was that! Not a single friendly word of encouragement for the perilous task he was about to begin. With a slight shrug Chris began the uninteresting process of eating and drinking the special food and liquid. Then, grimly, he snapped on his helmet, reported to control, and switched on the exhaust pump. When the vacuum was as nearly complete as possible, he swung open the hatch and prepared to leap outside.

Just as he was about to jump he remembered he had not yet thanked God for his safety so far. How easy it is, he thought remorsefully, to ask for divine protection and then, when you get it, to take it for granted. He offered up a silent prayer of thanksgiving and asked for help in the task ahead.

What was it he was going to face? Apart from the hazards of the journey and the deadly radioactivity caused by the destruction of the domes, would he have to contend with whoever had built the domes to attack the Earth? Chris shuddered as this staggering possibility struck him. After all, there was no reason to believe that the alien creatures who had so nearly conquered mankind were not present on the moon in some form, or that they had abandoned their aggressive intentions. Would he come into contact with those strange beings from another world? He would need all his courage to face what lay ahead.

[118]

Chris jumped easily from the side of the rocket. He had no difficulty now with the low lunar gravity, yet the strange experience was still sufficiently novel for him to enjoy it. Carefully judging an angle of fifteen degrees from the line of the shadow cast by Columbus, he noted a distant landmark toward which he would set course. Then, the oxygen cylinders fixed tightly to his back, he started off on his momentous voyage.

Chris soon found that he had to concentrate on the landmark ahead, for so many lunar features were the same. In about twenty minutes he had reached his object. He paused to take another sighting. Turning briefly, he saw the friendly shape of Columbus far away. He hoped that this wouldn't be his last sight of it! Very soon the rocket had disappeared from sight, and a sense of intense loneliness fell on him. Thank God for the voices of Uncle George and good old Whiskers, which sounded regularly in his helmet!

Twice he had a nasty scare. Landing at the end of a leap on what seemed to be a flat surface, he found himself sinking as far as his armpits into a shallow depression filled with dust. After that he distrusted the even ground and tried jumping from hillock to hillock. Each time he reached his target he took a fresh bearing, checked with his Geiger counter and reported back to Earth. Nowhere could he see any sign of the Russian rocket, though he realized that his horizon was so limited this could easily be just a few miles away.

After about two hours of steady progress Chris caught his first glimpse of the crater's edge. Even at a distance of some miles the mountains, though not particularly high, seemed grim and forbidding. The effect was heightened as he came nearer. Many of them rose from the crater floor as straight as a wall; others were a jumbled mass of twisted rock and rubble. He stopped at the foot. The mountains, seeming like something from a nightmare, shielded the crater from what lay beyond.

And what did lie beyond? Something from a remote universe? Something fearsome beyond imagining? Courageous though he was, Chris shook with apprehension as he stood at the foot of those great bastions. Could he make himself go on, or would his nerve fail him for this vital part of his task?

"I'm starting the climb now," he forced himself to report. He knew that if he hesitated any longer he would be lost; he might even return ignominiously to the rocket.

"Good for you!" Wing Commander Greatrex's cheerful voice came back. "They're letting me have a spell on the mike, Chris, so don't let my babbling worry you."

Worry me! thought Chris. Why, it's just what I need, bless him!

"You won't worry me," he called back more cheerfully than he felt. "I'm just concerned for fear your mustache will clog up the mike."

After further uncomplimentary remarks, Chris started the ascent. While some of the mountains rose like a cliff face, others had a gentler slope, and it was one of these that he selected. Several times during vacations he had done rock climbing, so the task ahead was not altogether strange to him. On Earth, however, he had never been encumbered with a space suit. On the other hand, he had never felt so light and strong. He had no doubt he could manage the ascent. What was worrying him was—what would he find on the other side?

The routine of Geiger checks continued, showing only a very slight increase in activity. Chris's greatest trouble was the brittle nature of some of the rock. He would grasp a suitable-looking piece to haul himself up, only to have it break off in his glove. After a time he found that the rocks which caused the most trouble were lighter in color than the others, so he avoided them as much as possible.

The first hour's climb was not too difficult. He must now be halfway to the top. Pausing for a short rest—though the ascent was taking surprisingly little effort—Chris turned to survey the plain of Plato that lay beneath him. In all directions lay the dust. Craters, crevasses, hillocks, and mounds made up the landscape as far as he could see. Glancing at his compass, Chris noted the direction of the needle which would be pointing toward Columbus. He strained his eyes to get a glimpse of this link with Mother Earth, but the rocket was too far away to be visible. Neither was the Soviet projectile anywhere in sight.

After a short rest Chris resumed his climb. He picked his way carefully upward, sometimes scrambling over loose stones split from the mountainside by the boiling hot days and freezing nights. Gradually he came nearer the ridge that ran along the highest point. On instructions from Sir George, who was now on control, Chris proceeded very cautiously.

Every five minutes he checked for radiation. When he reached a point a hundred feet or so below the ridge, the counter began to demand attention. With each foot he advanced, the light flashed more rapidly. If his suit had not been heavily protected against such a contingency, he could have gone no farther. As it was, with redoubled caution he scrambled to the brow of the mountain. From there he looked beyond, toward the region from which the strange beings from space had mounted their venomous attack on an unsuspecting Earth.

CHAPTER 12

As he peered ahead, Chris's heart was pounding with shock and apprehension. By now he had become more familiar with the lunar landscape, but here was a scene fantastic beyond description. It was as if he were looking inside a furnace that had grown cold. Everywhere rocks and dust had been fused by terrific heat into a substance that looked like black glass. This had heaved and twisted into all manner of shapes, each more weird than the last.

From flat areas like pools of shining jet, wickedly sharp teeth projected. Some of the molten rock had been lifted into thin folded sections, which looked for all the world like black velvet curtains. Nowhere was there anything more than a few feet high. Parts had been leveled flat as if by a giant steam-roller. The scene seemed like something from a vivid nightmare.

As well as he could, Christopher described what he saw. Now he must make his way through this horrible region in an endeavor to find traces of the mysterious buildings whose destruction had been the cause of this mighty holocaust. If he could find a fragment and return it to Earth for analysis, it might be possible to learn more about the creatures who had built the domes. Resolutely he began the descent. He found the going very difficult. Several times he slipped on the glassy rocks, and had it not been for the low gravity he might have been seriously injured. But whenever he fell, he did so as gently as a leaf falling from a tree.

It was more than eight hours after he had left Columbus before Chris completed the descent and stood on the vitrified plain. The radioactivity was now considerable, and control considered the advisability of allowing him to continue. However, as he had not yet found any dome fragments, Frayling decided he must go on.

Fortunately the radiation remained fairly constant. Chris moved forward, looking anxiously for any sign of the space beings or the remains of their work. The former site of the domes, near the Pico mountain, was many miles away. He could not hope to reach it in the time allotted, for in just over three hours he must turn back in order to reach the rocket within the twenty-four hours.

Chris now began to feel uncomfortably warm in his space suit. Perhaps it was the continuous exercise. It could not be the radiation, for he was well shielded to stand it—at least the intensity he had encountered so far. Unfortunately there was no shade in which he could pause to rest. All he could do was to go on. His conversation with control became less frequent and less cheerful. He did not feel tired. Maybe he was becoming a little feverish, Chris thought, for he noticed the suggestion of a headache. He must not crack up now, with the most vital part of his duty still ahead!

He plodded on, mile after mile. He was almost silent now. The pain in his head had increased, and he was feeling really ill. To the inquiries from control he invariably replied that he was all right. He wasn't going to let them think he was a quitter! But it was becoming more and more of an effort to concentrate attention sufficiently to keep up that sharp lookout. At times he felt as if he were going to faint. Only the thought that he would be letting down his friends gave him the will to carry on. Chris reflected that he had not felt like this for a long time, since—why, not since he was speeding over the same area in a rocket twelve months before!

That was it! As the memory of his previous adventure came back, he was convinced that what he could feel now had something to do with the malignant creatures whose work he had helped to destroy. So they were still present on the moon! At least, Chris thought, it seemed like it. With an effort he gave control a true account of his situation and his theory that the space beings were the cause. There was a slight delay before any reply came. Evidently a lively discussion was going on back on Earth. Then the order was transmitted.

"You are to return to Columbus at once."

That was it, then. He was to go no farther; he was to retreat back to the rocket without a fragment of dome structure. In other words, he'd failed!

The shame and disgust created by this idea caused a momentary return of strength. Darn control! He'd go on a bit farther even if it killed him. After all, it was his own life he was playing with. Unless he could get a sample, there wasn't much point in his returning to Earth. Control had received all the information he could give them over the radio. No, he'd go on till he dropped!

Steadying himself as best he could, Christopher lunged forward. He ignored the persistent requests for information that kept sounding in his ears. Time after time he fell on the glassy floor as the drumming in his head increased and he felt weaker. Each time he got to his feet with greater difficulty, but on he went. Both Sir George and Wing Commander Greatrex pleaded with him to tell them what was happening.

It grieved him to ignore his friends, but only by doing this could he hang on to the last shred of willpower that enabled him to go on.

Now he knew the end was near. He could barely raise himself up to stagger along. In any case, he knew he would not have the strength to change over to his third bottle of oxygen when his present one became exhausted—as it would be very soon. Oh, well, he had done his best. Perhaps the Russian had done better. No, he must crawl on. He raised his throbbing head in a last painful effort. Then he saw it!

The minitank moved steadily over the floor of Plato. Serge, too, had been told how to plot his course. Keenly he looked about him as he traveled on. Like his British counterpart, he found the lunar conditions strange and disturbing, yet exhilarating. It was good to be exploring the moon, with the whole Soviet nation awaiting reports of his progress. The only cloud on his horizon was the presence, somewhere, of the Western imperialist.

Several times Serge looked back to see the trail that the tracks of his vehicle were leaving in the dust. Down craterlet, over hillock, he was keeping a fairly straight course toward Plato's rim. His keen eyes peered right, left, and straight ahead.

Something unusual glinting in the powerful sunshine far to his right caught Serge's eye. Whatever it was, it was worth investigating. Announcing his intention over his radio, he swung the minitank round and headed toward the object of his curiosity.

It must have been several miles away, for it was almost a quarter of an hour before he seemed to be getting nearer. Rising to the top of a small mound, he caught a better view. His pulse started to race. It was the rocket—the imperialist's rocket! Five minutes later he was sure of it. He hurried on as quickly as the minitank would travel.

Columbus stood there deserted, its pilot miles away, near the crater's rim. Grimly Serge drove his vehicle around this symbol of the hated capitalists. Since no sign of life was visible, he warily approached nearer. It was undoubtedly deserted, he reported through his radio. He must act on his own initiative, the Communists told Serge, knowing full well how he had been carefully conditioned to act.

By giving Serge these orders, and making sure that the conversations were recorded, the Communists cleverly planned to avoid responsibility for what they knew inevitably must follow. They could scarcely be held responsible for the actions of a youth a quarter of a million miles away!

Act on his own initiative! Serge knew what that action would be. With grim pleasure he prepared his gun for its real task. Blast off samples of rock? This was much more important! He edged the minitank forward. The rocket was a sitting target, but he wanted to get a little closer to make sure of its destruction. At the top of a sharp little incline Serge halted the Russian vehicle and sighted his gun. Then, with a thrill of pleasure, the young Russian pressed the firing switch, for the glory of the Soviet Union.

There was a flash of flames from the little tank's gun, then the shining rocket—product of the finest brains in the Western world—tilted over still further, with a gaping hole in its casing. All was completely silent in this airless world. Columbus was damaged beyond repair. It would never more rise majestically into the heavens. It would never carry Chris Godfrey back to safety and his friends.

But where was the minitank? It had disappeared from view, as if whisked away by some magical power!

His senses reeling, Chris struggled toward the thing that had attracted his attention. From a distance it looked like a piece of silver shining in the intense light.

It was very visible against the darker ground of this burned and tortured region. Instinctively he knew that this was a fragment blasted from one of the mysterious domes, and that it was made of some element foreign to Earth.

This was what he had been sent for. If he could take this fragment back to Earth, it was as much as could be expected from this first expedition. He must get it and then try to make his way back to Columbus.

Several times Chris must have lost consciousness. His oxygen supply was getting perilously low, and the queer sensations in his head had increased. It took all his willpower to force himself forward over the last fifty yards. Would he never reach the shining thing? Had it not been for the low gravity, Chris could never have crawled those final few feet. How he did it he never knew, but at last the bright fragment was within reach.

It was even an effort to remember his instructions as to what he must do now. He knew that he must not touch it by hand, and that he must put it into the lead container he had brought along for that purpose. From his belt he tugged a pair of tongs, unclipped them, and opened the lid of the lead container. Fearfully he reached out toward this strange piece of matter, the like of which no man had seen before.

He could see now that it was luminous, and that the light it gave out was its own. It seemed to be flat and about an inch thick. At first he wondered whether it would fit into the lead box. Should he try to break it into small pieces? He seized it with the tongs and tried to lift it up, but it would not move. He tried again, using more effort. This time he did manage to stir it.

The dome fragment was as heavy as lead—that is, as heavy as lead would be on Earth. It took all Chris's fast-ebbing strength to inch it forward toward the container. With relief he saw that it would just about fit inside, for he felt sure that nothing he could do would break this strange substance.

At last it was in! The glowing fragment lay safely in the dark metal box. By the time he'd sealed the container, Chris was utterly exhausted. He must have passed out as soon as he had completed his task. The next he remembered he was lying flat on the lunar floor, gasping for breath. Quite clearly he knew he was dying—unless he could get more oxygen within the next few seconds.

A great fatigue came over him. Why not give up the struggle and pass out forever? He was sure he could never get back to the rocket. But first he would like to have one more word with Uncle George and old Whiskers. What about his radio, though? It had been silent for some time. Had it broken down?

Chris's effort to speak was more of a choking sound than any intelligible word. Still the loudspeaker was silent. Perhaps he was out of range of his rocket's transmitter and so the vital link with control was broken. Now his friends would never know what had happened to him and how nearly he had succeeded in his task. If—if he could just get enough oxygen to crawl back into range!

Red lights were flashing in his eyes and waterfalls were thundering in his ears as he fumbled feebly with the valves which controlled the life-giving gas. In his agony he prayed that he might have one last word with his friends, and receive one last message of comfort before his life came to an end.

How it happened he had no idea, but oxygen from a fresh cylinder began to flow strongly into his helmet. In his own mind Chris had no doubt that this was the work of the divine Providence which had saved him so often before.

Right from the first long gulps, he began to feel better. As he breathed the oxygen gratefully into his lungs he wondered whether, after all, he should not make the effort to get back to Columbus. Perhaps it was God's intention that he should return with the fruits of his labors and not perish miserably on this lonely world. The buzzing in his head was no better, but this condition would improve, he knew, if he could get away from this ghastly area.

Full of a new determination, Christopher took the first steps back over the way he had come. If his outward journey had been difficult, the return was doubly so, encumbered as he now was with the heavy substance in the container. For half an hour he struggled on in a desperate effort to reach the base of the mountains. His progress was slow, but every minute the queer feeling in his head bothered him less. His confidence began to grow.

Periodically he would try the radio, but it still remained silent. He tried to remember just where it was that he had received his last message from Earth, but he could not. If it was after he had reached the fused area, he should soon be picking up control again.

The mountains were quite near now. How he longed to be over them and down the other side in the comparatively friendly region of Plato! It was going to be difficult to lug the heavy container up some of the slopes, but he had brought it so far he was determined not to be beaten now. So he began the grueling climb.

Never had Chris felt so exhausted. At fairly frequent intervals he was compelled to rest and to let his laboring heart quiet down. His consumption of oxygen must be prodigious. Anxiously he watched the gauges. Each time he paused he would try to make radio contact with control, but all was silent. Puzzled and worried, a sense of isolation began to creep over him.

By the time he reached the top of the mountain rim he was on his last oxygen cylinder. Many times he had been tempted to abandon his burden, but had resisted the impulse. Now the going should be easier. If only he could get something over the radio! Anyway, his radar compass was all right; the needle pointed steadily toward where he knew Columbus was waiting. And thank goodness his head was clear again, being shielded from the strange power of the space creatures by the friendly ramparts of Plato.

The rocket could not be too far away now. Soon he should be able to catch sight of its comforting outline. As he followed the trail he'd made in the dust on the way out, his eyes sought eagerly for the first glimpse of it. It would be good to get back into the familiar cabin and rest his weary body on the contour couch. Then control could arrange the take-off as soon as possible. He would be glad to be speeding homeward!

Chris stopped dead in his tracks. There was the rocket, but even from a distance something about its appearance was disquietingly strange. In deepening anxiety he pushed on. As he got closer his dismay increased. He could see there was something wrong, very wrong, with Columbus. It was leaning drunkenly, and there was a gaping hole in its side. With painful clarity Chris saw that the rocket—his only means of return—was damaged beyond hope of repair. He was marooned forever on this barren satellite!

He sank down in an agony of despair. Within a matter of hours he would be dead, his life wasted in utter loneliness. Well, perhaps not wasted altogether. At least control had recorded his reports, which would perhaps be useful to those who came after him. But what had happened to Columbus? What had caused the damage to its hull? A meteor? Chris raised himself to look again at the damaged rocket. Finally he got to his feet and staggered toward it.

Now that he was nearer, Chris could see that the hole went right through the missile. Whatever had struck it had entered one side of the casing and passed out through the opposite side. The metal was turned along the edges of the holes, clearly showing which way the penetration had taken place. In a blinding flash he knew that it could not have been a meteor which had struck Columbus.

A meteor would not travel on a path parallel to the ground and so near the surface. It would have struck the rocket from above, or at least its passage through the hull would have been a downward one, not like that indicated by the two holes. If not a meteor, what then? An even colder chill gripped Chris's heart. Could it—could it be the Russian? Had the pilot of the Soviet rocket discovered Columbus during Chris's absence and deliberately destroyed it?

Surely such a thing was incredible. Yet Chris knew the deep animosity with which the Communists regarded this Western venture. And what other explanation was there? He knew now why his loudspeaker had been silent. The apparatus in the rocket had been put out of action. This was the reason his friends had not spoken to him! And now he would not be able to report this disaster to control.

They would never know on Earth what had happened to him—unless, he thought ruefully, they heard from the Russian pilot. He would lie on the contour couch and compose himself as best he could until his oxygen ran out. Of course there were several full cylinders inside, if they had not been destroyed. But they could only prolong his life by a few hours. Better get it over and done with.

Wearily he climbed up the sloping side of the vehicle till he came to the open hatch. He pulled himself inside dejectedly and looked around. It took some minutes to assess the extent of the damage. Whatever had struck Columbus had passed through it, smashing many of its instruments but missing the oxygen supply. The radio, too, seemed intact until he looked at it more closely. Then he saw that the cable from the batteries had been severed.

What if he could repair it? Would the radio work again? If only it would! Dying so many thousands of miles away from his friends would not be so bad if only he could hear their voices. He clipped on a fresh oxygen cylinder and examined the cable more closely.

The break caused by the object which had passed through was about a foot long, for that length of cable had been carried clean away. How to bridge the gap? He must get wire from somewhere and try to join it to the broken ends. There was no spare cable in the cabin, so he must take a piece from one of the other instrument leads. It doesn't matter which one, Chris thought a little bitterly as he wrenched away a length which he knew carried power to the fuel pumps.

There were no suitable tools at hand, naturally. Even the coldly calculating brain of Sir Leo Frayling had failed to foresee such a situation as the one in which Chris now found himself. He succeeded in baring the cable ends by rubbing them against the jagged side of the gaping hole. Could he join the loose piece to the two broken ends and so bridge the gap?

Working with gloved hands made the job extremely difficult, and for a long time Chris fumbled at it without success. Only by persistent effort did he finally manage to make the last connection. Then he knew the struggle had been worthwhile. The loudspeaker in his helmet came alive, and he could hear human voices. Fearful lest this precarious link should be broken, he almost hesitated to speak.

"Hello! Hello!" he called in a strangled voice. "Can you hear me?"

There was a confusion of sound from the other end, and a terrific crackling noise showed how poor was the electrical connection he'd made. But he could make out Sir George's words. "Christopher! Thank God you've come through! What's happened? We haven't had a sound out of you for seven hours. Are you all right?"

"I'm all right," Chris managed to say, "but Columbus has been damaged. There's a hole right through the hull, and the radio was put out too."

"Great Heavens! What—what's happened?" Benson gasped.

As clearly as he could, Chris gave the scientist an account of what he had found on his return to the rocket. He told why he believed it impossible for the hole to have been made by a meteor.

There was consternation in control as the scientists and engineers realized the significance of what had been said. So the Russians had done it, had they? Could Chris get any proof of this? Were there any signs around that the Soviet pilot had been near?

Chris promised to go out and investigate.

Frayling's voice was as cold and unemotional as ever when he took over the mike. He questioned Godfrey closely about the extent and nature of the damage. Then came his instructions.

"You have no doubt realized that Columbus cannot return to Earth. We can do nothing to help you. It is imperative that you use what oxygen you have left to establish Russian complicity. If you do this beyond doubt it will be an international incident of the gravest kind. Now Benson wants to speak to you again."

"Chris—" the voice of his friend sounded unnatural and he could tell that Sir George was laboring under the stress of great emotion—"I just don't know what to say, lad."

"It's all right, Uncle George," Chris answered. He didn't know whether he'd concealed the choking feeling he had in his throat. "It's all right. It had to come sometime. I'm going outside now to have a look round."

Without waiting for a reply, Chris went to the hatch and climbed down. He hadn't the heart now to jump as he had done before. When he reached the ground he stood for a moment and looked sadly at the crippled rocket. Then he turned and set out to find signs of the Russian.

CHAPTER 13

Christopher knew that he had, with the reserve supply in the rocket, enough oxygen to last another fourteen hours. After that—well, he would just fade out. He might as well do what he could in the short time left to find out the cause of the damage. Besides, it would occupy his mind and keep morbid thoughts at bay. If in the end his nerve cracked, he would smash his radio so that his friends would never know. But first he would see what he could find.

From a careful look at the holes in the hull, Chris could easily tell the direction from which whatever had pierced it had come. He set off on this bearing, carefully scanning the ground as he went. Crossing the area of bare rock from which poor old Columbus had blasted the dust, he came to the covered area where the blue-gray powder was still performing its strange little dance.

He kept up a commentary to control with forced cheerfulness, and Benson or Greatrex replied in the same manner. Climbing a slight rise about a hundred yards from his starting point, he let out a startled shout.

There, in a hollow on the other side, he saw what he knew at once was the Russian tank!

He retreated rapidly down the rise. As he crouched in the dust, out of sight, he described his discovery over the radio. There could be no doubt now that the Communist pilot had attacked and damaged the rocket.

The gravity with which Chris's discovery was received was unmistakable, for this incident could not fail to create an East-West crisis. Even as Chris was still crouching in the dust, Frayling was speaking into a telephone with the news that would inflame the Western world.

What was he to do now? Chris asked. Sir George Benson advised him to exercise the utmost caution. It was quite evident that the Russian pilot was hostile and armed.

As he listened to Sir George's words, Chris smiled grimly to himself. After all, what use was there in being cautious? He had only a little over thirteen hours to live, in any case. Though he had no wish to cause his best friend more distress, he decided he must take another peep. What puzzled him was why the Russian tank was still there. Why, having completed the rocket's destruction, had it not moved off on its own mission? Surely it was not waiting quietly for him to return to Columbus. That would be a terrific waste of oxygen. What was it doing, then, concealed in this hollow?

Chris began a slow crawl up the rise. How strange, he thought, that there was no need to worry about making a noise! At the top he raised his head carefully and had another look.

There was no sign of any movement from the little tank. If the Russian inside had seen him, he wasn't doing anything about it. As Chris looked more carefully at the little tank, something remarkable about it struck him. Its tracks were on top and not in contact with the ground beneath. How could it move like that?

In a flash the answer came to him. It could not move; it was lying on its back, helpless.

Excited at his discovery, Chris raised himself up a little. Quite close to him he saw in the dust the marks left by the tank. It seemed to have fallen over backward from the rim of the depression. It must have done this after it had attacked Columbus, for it certainly could not have attacked it from where it lay now.

Chris had guessed the truth. As Serge had fired at his target, something unexpected happened. The recoil from the shot was sufficient, under the low gravity, to turn the minitank over. Now it lay like a helpless beetle on its back.

"What shall I do now?" Chris asked after he had reported what he'd found. Control could not give him a definite answer, except to suggest that he try to find out if the occupant of the vehicle was still alive.

Warily Chris examined his find. He would first locate the sting in the "beetle" and then keep well away from it. With the utmost care he approached the tank and began to make his way slowly around it. Could the Russian inside—if he was still conscious—detect his presence? That was something he'd have to risk. Ah, that must be a gun! Yes, it certainly looked as if he'd found the offensive part of the tank.

"I believe it's wedged," Chris murmured over his radio as he peered at the gun. It certainly seemed as if the weight of the minitank rested largely on the projecting tube of the weapon. If so, it couldn't be swiveled around and would be practically useless from the position it was in. Boldly, now, though keeping away from the nozzle of the gun, Chris walked right up to the side of the tank and struck at the metal with his armored shoe. He knew this would not create any sound, unless the Russian was in a free atmosphere inside the tank. But the reverberations of his kick should get through to him and let him know that someone was outside.

Chris was right. His action had certainly revealed his presence to the person in the vehicle, for the tracks began to run uselessly over their wheels. Chris could see plainly that it was quite impossible for the Soviet tank ever to move, as long as it remained in that position. He wondered what control would tell him to do.

There was just about twelve and a half hours left.

As Serge had fired his gun at the imperialist rocket the front of his tank reared up. It was already at an angle of some thirty degrees, due to the climb up the side of the depression. Now the vehicle turned completely over, flinging the young man from the controls. Dazed, he picked himself up. He soon realized what had happened, but it was not until he tried to move the tank that he discovered the true extent of the disaster. He was unable to move, imprisoned in a tiny vehicle on an airless world!

To his great credit, Serge did not lose his nerve. He reported calmly to his headquarters what had happened. To anyone from the Western world, what followed would seem unbelievable. Serge was greeted with a torrent of abuse for having been so careless as to put the minitank out of action. The destruction of the imperialist's rocket was not commented on, or that Serge would remain there to die a slow death. The important thing to the Communist officials was that the opportunity to bring off a great technical achievement, with tremendous propaganda value, had been lost.

Now the Soviet Union was no farther ahead than the Western powers. The capitalists had on the moon an active pilot and an immobilized rocket; the U.S.S.R., an undamaged rocket and a pilot out of action. Could anything be more damaging to Soviet prestige, with all the world waiting to see the triumphant return of the rocket Lenin?

Serge accepted the rebukes and accusations meekly, with no thought that perhaps he did not deserve such harsh reprimands, or that, if he had made a mistake, he would probably shortly be paying for it with his life.

Serge was ordered to do all in his power to get the minitank operative again. Could he perhaps turn it on its side? He knew that it would be instant death if he were to try and open the door, for he had no space suit. Perhaps if he flung himself against the side of the tank he might be able to move it. He could not think of any other way of dislodging it from its present position.

Desperately Serge hurled his body at a blank space on the side of the tank. The force of the impact shook the vehicle, but it settled back as it was before. Again and again he threw his bruised body against the side, but it was useless. Although he could rock the vehicle appreciably, he could not turn it over.

Now he sank down, battered and exhausted, a prey to black despair. He could only wait for the slow, inevitable suffocation that must follow. If only—though it seemed treason to think it—if only he hadn't blasted at the Western rocket!

Periodically Serge roused himself from the lethargy into which he kept sinking, to have another futile attempt at turning the tank over, though common sense told him he was wasting his strength and his oxygen. Nothing but abuse sounded over his radio; he was even accused of deliberate sabotage of this glorious Soviet undertaking. Serge listened in bitter silence. What was the good of replying? Nothing could alter the fact that he was imprisoned in an upturned tank in a barren world, a quarter of a million miles away from the help of any other human—except perhaps the Western pilot, who must be likewise doomed. Was it all worthwhile?

How long he lay in a state of semi-stupor, Serge did not know. He must have dozed or lost consciousness for a time, when he suddenly became fully alive. He had heard a sound!

There was no doubt about it. It wasn't his imagination. A definite sound had come from the wall of the tank, as if it had been struck from the outside. For a moment Serge's heart beat wildly. Possible explanations flooded into his head, the most probable being that a meteorite had struck the vehicle. He sank down again despondently, then rose as another thought occurred to him. Could it be that the Westerner had found him? If so, he must reply in some way. Serge started the tracks of the tank and waited breathlessly for the result.

When Chris saw this definite sign of life, he kicked the tank again. Inside, Serge heard the noise, and now he could have no doubt. A choking lump rose to his throat as he realized that another human being—even if it was the hated imperialist pilot—was only a couple of feet away from him. He banged back on the metal side, then stopped as he realized that the sound of his blow could not reach the other because of the vacuum outside. Several times he restarted the tank tracks to indicate that the signals had been heard.

Both young men at the same time reported the encounter to their respective controls. What, each of them asked, was he to do?

When the Western governments, through Sir Leo Frayling, had heard of the Communist attack on their rocket ship, tension immediately rose to danger point. There were those in each of the governments who advocated an immediate declaration of war in reply to this act of aggression. Only with the greatest difficulty did the more cautious statesmen prevail upon their belligerent colleagues. Never had the world been closer to the fury of an atomic war. It had needed only a single command for firing buttons to be pressed in scores of rocket sites to set in motion devastation impossible even to imagine.

When the two young men on the moon asked for instructions on what to do next, the Western and Eastern governments were unable to decide. Consultations were taking place constantly by means of radio, but no decision was arrived at by either side. There was a complete impasse, and the longer it lasted the more dangerous it became.

Knowing nothing of this situation on Earth, Chris examined the position of the minitank in more detail, always keeping well away from the gun. It was clear that, unless it was dislodged, the Russian vehicle would never move again. This would mean that the man inside would perish as surely as he himself would die. Two lives would be wasted, and the all-important dome fragment would never reach Earth. How silly it all seemed! But for the animosity between their governments, both of them would probably have made a safe journey home, and an important step would have been taken toward finding out more about the builders of the domes.

Inside the tank, Serge was beginning to think along similar lines. What had his attempt to destroy the Western rocket achieved? Only the failure of both East and West in their lunar expeditions. If he had not attacked the imperialist's rocket, he could by now have explored much of the moon's surface. Perhaps he might have discovered something about the space creatures. Now, all that great effort by his country was wasted. It was all so— He pulled himself up with a start. Such traitorous thoughts were a crime against the State! Yet was it a crime to wish that the expedition had succeeded and that his own life had been saved?

Gradually Christopher came to a conclusion. By chipping away one small lump of rock and by pushing as hard as he could at the side, the minitank, he was certain, could be righted. After all, its weight would not be very great. He suggested this to Sir Leo Frayling in control.

"You are to attempt nothing of the kind without instructions," the chief scientist's cold voice snapped back.

"It might make it possible for one of us to get back with the dome fragment," Chris argued.

"We are not prepared to let the Communists succeed alone," Frayling barked.

"So neither of us succeeds?" the young man asked bitterly.

A new voice came over the radio. On Earth his words had been heard by the small group of tired and strained men who could not tear themselves away from this last contact with the doomed youth. As Chris had reported his opinion, the eyes in the haggard face of Sir George Benson lit as an idea entered his mind. Looking up, he caught the glances of Wing Commander Greatrex and Dr. Rosenberg, neither of whom would leave control during these tragic hours. Had they had the same thought? They had!

"It is a chance in a million," the American whispered to the other two, "but that's better than no chance at all."

Though all three of Chris's friends realized that Frayling would veto their scheme, Benson urgently beckoned him away from the microphone.

"Look, Frayling," Benson said in a low voice, "Rosenberg, Greatrex, and I believe it's worth having Christopher try to free the minitank if the Russians will agree to bring him back to Earth in their rocket. What do you say?"

For a moment the chief scientist looked at Benson incredulously.

"I think you're crazy!" he snapped at last, turning back to the mike.

He found a burly figure with a bristling ginger mustache barring his way. The Wing Commander's usually ruddy face was now pale with the intensity of his feelings. He seized the chief scientist's arm in a grip that made him wince with pain.

"If there's a chance of bringing young Chris back alive, you're not going to stand in the way," he snarled.

The startled Frayling looked at him and at the other

two. Their stern, set faces stared at him implacably. He could read a desperate determination in their eyes. For a moment more he hesitated. Then he said, "Very well, try it. What the effect will be on the international situation I can't predict, but I want to get hold of the dome fragment."

"The international situation can't be much worse," Rosenberg pointed out. "This may even improve it."

The decision taken, Frayling handed the microphone over to Sir George while he spoke urgently over the radio telephone to London. Soon there was frenzied diplomatic activity in a half-dozen world capitals as statesmen consulted desperately together.

Meantime, Benson was saying, "Chris, if you think there's a chance of rescuing the minitank, we'll bargain with the Russians to bring you back in their rocket. Hold everything for the moment, though. Things are moving quickly here. Frayling's speaking to London now, but I'm afraid it will be some time before we can get agreement, even if it's technically possible. How much oxygen is left?"

"About enough for another six hours."

"Right. Now go back to Columbus. Relax on the contour couch to save as much oxygen as possible. We'll keep in touch all the time. Can you make it?"

"Yes, I can get back into the cabin. But look, Uncle George, even if they can't squeeze me into the Russian rocket, don't you think I ought to help their chap get back with the fragment?"

"We'll face that situation when we come to it," Benson answered. "Now off you go, Chris. Just let us know when you've settled down. After that, don't even speak unless it is absolutely necessary."

"Anything you say, though I'm not very hopeful," the young man said. "I wish you'd let me push this chap onto his tracks again."

He gave one more thump on the vehicle, then made

his way back to his damaged rocket. He sighed at the sight of Columbus standing forlorn and lonely, never again to rise majestically on top of a long tail of flame. Then, with what patience he could muster, he climbed into the cabin and settled down to await his fate.

CHAPTER 14

While Chris was lying inert to conserve his oxygen, things were certainly very hectic down on Earth. With the vital minutes ticking away relentlessly, every second was important. The various governments behind Operation Columbus were agreed that they would co-operate with the Soviet Union rather than sacrifice the results of both expeditions, to say nothing of the two young men. Would Russia agree as well? And if so, could the Communists be trusted? There was much heart searching among the statesmen of the West before the fateful message was sent.

The Western offer of co-operation took the Kremlin by surprise. Was this some plot of the imperialists to undermine the results of Soviet technical achievement? What would be the effect of this co-operation on the uncommitted nations? Could the imperialists be trusted? Had there been more time, there is little doubt that the Soviet leaders would have studied the message for the best ways to obtain from it the maximum political advantage. As it was, a decision had to be made quickly.

It was Boronoff who urged the Soviet leaders to accept the Western offer. He reminded them of his previous experience of working alongside scientists from the other side of the Iron Curtain. Had there not been full co-operation some twelve months earlier, the harmful radiation would never have been eliminated and civilization would by now have been destroyed. After all, he asked, what was there to lose from accepting the Western proposal? The rocket Lenin would be landed in the Soviet Union, brought home by the Russian guidance system.

It wasn't quite as easy as Boronoff pictured it. The Western governments insisted on having representatives in the landing area when the rocket returned. Russia countered by claiming a share of the dome fragment. Eventually, after many exchanges, which lasted more than four nerve-wracking hours, agreement was reached, and the scientists of both East and West were authorized to salvage what they could from the two ill-fated lunar expeditions.

As the hours dragged slowly on, Chris lay with what patience he could muster, carefully husbanding his precious oxygen supply. Sometimes he was filled with hope, but for the most part he felt a calm resignation to the fate which he believed lay in store for him. One resolve, however, he made, though he kept it to himself. Whatever the outcome of the negotiations on Earth, he would return good for evil—he would, if he could, push the minitank back and give his Russian rival a chance.

Periodically the voice of Sir George Benson or of Greatrex would come over the radio to cheer and encourage him. They relayed to him the latest news of the political negotiations which meant so much to him. Silently Christopher laid his own plans. He would wait as long as possible for the people back on Earth to see the sense of working together. If they failed to agree, he would use his last hour of life to help the Russian chap. At last, when he was almost convinced that this was the only thing left for him to do, his radio crackled and Sir Leo Frayling told him that agreement had been reached.

For some time Serge had heard no sound from the Western pilot on the moon outside. His nerves now tightly strung, Serge listened intently for a sign. He felt incredibly lonely and abandoned. It was useless, he knew, to expect any sympathy from his radio. The messages from Earth had left him in little doubt that his masters held him responsible for the expedition's failure. If he could have it to do over again, he would keep well away from the other lunar explorer; certainly he wouldn't attack him. How he wished his end would come quickly! Still, he would like to hear the other man again before he passed out.

Had the Westerner already succumbed to lack of oxygen? Serge guessed that his supply was more limited than his own. Perhaps even now his rival was lying outside the vehicle, his last conscious act having been to tap the message of his presence to his fellow victim. Alone, unobserved, Serge was able to indulge in the unusual luxury of regretting what he had done. A lump rose to his throat and his eyes closed in an ecstasy of self-reproach.

Hours passed, and then the long-silent radio spoke again. Its words had to be repeated many times before their significance began to sink into his bewildered mind. The Western governments had agreed that the pilot of the other rocket should try to turn the mini-tank back onto its tracks again so that it could move about once more. If the effort was successful, Serge was to return at once to Lenin, taking the Westerner with him.

A glow of hope spread through the Russian. So perhaps after all he would not die on this eerie world! Perhaps he, and the Westerner too, would be able to get back to Earth once more. For some time he was incapable of thinking calmly, so great was the tumult within him. What had come over the Kremlin that it had agreed to this capitalist co-operation? It was contrary to all his carefully guided thinking and was very confusing. But that was not his problem at the moment. His task was to work with the Westerner in a desperate effort to save them both.

Chris received Frayling's announcement with relief. Whether or not he himself was saved mattered less than that there was a good chance for one pilot to return safely, bringing the dome fragment. Grimly he checked his oxygen supply. There would be time to right the tank, unless it proved to be a more difficult task than he anticipated. But whether there was also enough oxygen to get to the Russian rocket was doubtful. At Sir Leo's command he swung himself from the couch. What a relief it was to be active at last!

With a lighter heart than he had had for many hours, Chris jumped from the hatch. He was determined to savor as long as possible the exhilarating effect of the lunar gravity. With enthusiastic leaps he quickly covered the ground to the stricken tank and gave it a resounding knock. The signal was heard and the lively way the tracks moved in response seemed to indicate that the fellow inside had learned what was to happen.

There was no need now to fear a hostile gun. Chris made a careful examination all the way round to pick out the most likely direction in which he could turn over the vehicle. Going to the opposite side, he put his gloved hands on the metal and gave it an experimental push. The minitank moved a little, but then sank back into its old position.

On Earth the Russian vehicle would probably have weighed almost a ton, but here its comparative weight would be only about three hundredweights. Chris gave it a much harder push, which tilted the tank through several degrees before it fell back. H'm, this wasn't going to be too easy! Gathering all his strength, Chris pushed the metal until every sinew in his body protested.

It was no good. The minitank leaned encouragingly, but not enough to fall over. Was he going to fail after all? Chris felt bitterly disappointed as he relaxed again. How could he possibly do better? In fact, his strength would likely get less. Was there anything the chap inside could do? Shift as much weight as possible to the lee side? But how could he let the Russian know?

Reporting his failure to control, Chris suggested that if the weight inside the tank could be moved, he might be more successful. Neither he nor anyone at Woomera could communicate with the Russian directly, as his radio worked on a different wave length from Chris's. Any message would have to be beamed to the Soviet scientists, who would then transmit it to their rocket on the moon.

As he waited for this process, Chris fretted at the delay. Here he was, close to the man inside, yet all communication had to make a fantastic journey over thousands of miles and through many hands. Somehow there seemed something symbolic about this difficulty in getting a message to his opposite number on the other side of a metal sheet! A valuable ten minutes was wasted while his message made its tortuous way to the Russian pilot and the acknowledgement traveled back.

This time Chris failed by only a hair's breadth to topple the tank over. He sank in despair alongside the vehicle. Must he admit defeat? It would be a bitter blow, when success had seemed so near. As he was recovering from his exertions the radio spoke again. This time it was to say that if he would try again, the man inside would hurl himself against the side in an effort to help. He had reported that he had already rocked the tank by his own efforts.

Right! If this doesn't do the trick, thought Chris,

nothing ever will! Speaking into his mike, he asked that the Russian should wait till he felt the minitank tip, and then he should throw himself against the side when the tank was at the maximum angle. He would wait ten minutes before making this last desperate effort, to allow time for the Russians to contact their pilot. Chris emphasized that since he would not be able to hold up the tank for more than a couple of seconds, the Soviet man must be ready.

As the minutes ticked by, Christopher wondered what the fellow inside was feeling. What kind of chap was he? The fact that he had deliberately put Columbus out of action had almost vanished from Chris's mind. Now they were two human beings marooned on a desolate satellite, two young men whose only hope of salvation was a combined effort. If everything failed, Chris knew that he would spend the last minutes of his life tapping on the vehicle to try to give comfort to its occupant. Perhaps, in return, the Russian chap would wiggle his tracks!

Time now for the crucial trial. Chris stood up, placed his gloved hands under the corner of the tank, and took a deep breath. Muttering a silent prayer, Chris heaved—heaved as he never had done before, till every fiber of his body shrieked protest. Would the strain never cease? Time seemed to stand still. Then, magically, it was all over. The minitank toppled over, and Chris sprawled forward across it, semiconscious.

It must have been only seconds later when he felt the machine move. Now safely on his tracks, the Russian inside was joyfully trying them out. With Chris perched on top, the vehicle rose bravely up the side of the depression which had so nearly been its grave. From the way in which it turned round when it reached level ground, the young Briton guessed that the Russian was looking for him, anxious to catch sight of his nearest fellow creature, his rescuer.

The minitank stopped as if puzzled. Then Chris

realized that the Russian did not know he was on top. It must have seemed that he had vanished after accomplishing his task. To make his presence known, Chris thumped on the top of the vehicle, which immediately waltzed around in happy acknowledgement.

Without loss of time, the minitank set off in what Chris assumed was the direction of the rocket Lenin. Now at last he could relax a little. He sank down on top of the vehicle, grateful for the chance to rest his tortured muscles.

Suddenly he sat bolt upright. He'd forgotten to collect the dome fragment! He had left it, sealed in its container, somewhere between Columbus and the place where he had discovered the minitank. What should he do? He was now perhaps a mile from the starting point. By the time he got a message through to the chap in the tank they would have traveled at least another couple of miles. His oxygen was now definitely running low. It could last little more than half an hour. Why not forget the piece of mysterious material and scurry off to the Russian rocket as quickly as possible? Would anyone blame him, under the circumstances?

To this last question Chris knew there was a certain answer. He would never forgive himself if he did not try to recover the fragment! But how? Knocks on top of the tank would convey nothing to the driver except that he was still up there. Yet he must get the vehicle to go back with him, or he would never find Lenin on his own, even if the oxygen held out that long. There was only one way. It was risky, but he must do it.

Chris leaped forward off the tank, right in the path of its advance. Only by doing this could he be sure that the Russian would see him. How he missed being crushed beneath the tracks, Chris never knew. Fortunately the Russian's reactions were quick. The tank slewed round, missing Chris by a hair's breadth, then stopped.

Chris went forward to peer into the observation slit

and to try and convey to the Soviet pilot his wish to return. The slit was only about six inches high and two feet wide, so he was unable to see much of the man inside. He did catch sight of his face, however, looking angrily, it seemed, through the thick glass. Chris could almost hear him thinking: what is this Western fool doing, trying to commit suicide?

Urgently, with a wealth of gesture, Chris tried to make the Russian understand what he wanted. In return he received a series of signs that meant nothing to him. How could these two young men tell each other, the one that he must return for the dome fragment; the other that his batteries were running low, when they used different wave lengths and each spoke a language the other did not know?

Indeed, Serge was getting quite concerned, for his instruments showed him that he had used up a great deal of power in his early attempts to move the tank. Now this crazy Westerner had jumped off in front of him and seemed to be trying to prevent the tank from returning to Lenin. The idiot was pointing the way back to the imperialists' rocket and was moving as if he wanted to return to it.

Should he let the fool go and then make his way to possible safety with all speed? But the Western chap had turned over the tank and saved him, so he deserved some consideration. Besides, it seemed that the two of them were now to co-operate in the final stages of this venture. Though greatly worried about his power supply, Serge headed the minitank in the direction indicated, and Chris once more rode on top.

Anxiously the British youth scanned the ground ahead. Fortunately their tracks were easily visible in the lunar dust, so they came back to the almost-fatal depression with no difficulty. Thumping on top of the tank, Chris leaped off and signaled to his colleague to wait. He followed his own footprints, and in two minutes his search was over. With the heavy container firmly in his grasp, Chris returned to the waiting tank. Putting his burden down, he shaped his hands like a dome, then pointed to the container at his feet.

The watching Russian understood. He, too, had been instructed to bring back a fragment, but unlike the Westerner he had failed. But this wouldn't be too bad if, between them, they could bring one piece back to Earth! Serge gave a sign through his observation slit that he understood, and motioned his colleague to remount the tank. Chris placed the heavy object safely on top of the vehicle, then scrambled up himself. Once more Serge started off toward his rocket.

As he lay flat on the minitank, Chris's breath came in gasps. He knew this was not due to the exertion of lifting up the lead container. The last of his oxygen in the cylinder must have been used up and he now had only what was inside his helmet. So this was the end, after all! Well, at least the Soviet pilot might get back with the valuable and mysterious object of their search. A pity he had forgotten the container when the tank first started off. If he hadn't, his oxygen might have lasted. Ah, well, he might as well use the last bit saying farewell to Uncle George and the others.

Breathing painfully, the young man managed to speak into his microphone. The anxious voices from Earth came back. He must hold on; the Russian was being told of the situation and instructed how to get the life-saving gas to Chris as soon as the tank was sealed inside the Russian rocket. In order not to distress his friends, Chris pretended to be encouraged. They could not know how near to the end he was. Already his senses were swimming so that he was barely conscious of the moving vehicle. Still, he managed to choke out something like a cheery expression before blackness came upon him.

Serge, like Chris, bitterly regretted the false start without the fragment. Now it was a gamble whether he would have sufficient power to get back to Lenin.

Would his batteries last out? As he nursed the minitank carefully forward, his radio told him of the dire straits of the young man lying just above his head, and the action he must take on getting back into the rocket. The Russian's lips set grimly. Would he get to the rocket?

Yard after yard the vehicle staggered forward. Occasionally it stopped for a few seconds and Serge's heart rose to his mouth. Then it would surge forward again ever nearer the Soviet missile. Stop. Start. Stop. Start. Lenin was now less than half a mile away. The nerve-wracking journey continued. There was no sound from the Westerner, so it seemed likely that he had passed out. Could the tank make it to the rocket in time to save him? Serge hoped most fervently that it would; he wanted to repay his debt.

Only fifty yards to go now, and the minitank stopped again. Straight ahead Serge could see the open hatch and the ramp up which the vehicle must climb. Could he do it? Even if it reached the ramp, would the tank be able to climb it? He felt another flood of relief as he moved forward a few more precious yards.

Stop. Start. He was almost there now, and the suspense was becoming unendurable. It would be just too cruel if he failed when so near. Stop. Start. That was it! He'd reached the ramp. Now would it continue up? No, it wouldn't. The tank stopped again.

What could he do? He couldn't leave the vehicle. He would die instantly if he tried to open the door. Was he to remain there so tantalizingly near safety? And what about the poor chap on top? Frantically Serge manipulated the controls. It was no good. He sank onto his seat in despair. The next second he'd been shaken off onto the floor of the tank as it lurched forward and climbed slowly—oh, so slowly—up the ramp.

Would it make it? Serge held his breath. And what about the Westerner on the top outside? Would he be scraped off when the tank entered the rocket? The margin was small, as the aperture was very little larger than the vehicle itself. He hoped the chap was lying flat on top. Steadily the minitank crawled on. It was as if it was using its dying strength to creep home. At last it was inside. Now Serge faced the urgent task of seeing what had happened to his colleague.

Using the mechanical arm, Serge pushed the button which would raise the ramp and seal the rocket. In the slow, agonizing seconds while the operation was being completed, he stammered out a message over his radio. The very second he was sure the job was done he pushed another button—one he would not normally use—to allow oxygen to enter the compartment holding the vehicle. Then, without waiting for the pressure outside to reach its correct level, he unfastened the tank door.

He was almost flung outside by the escape of air. Gasping painfully, he squeezed himself into the narrow space between the vehicle and the compartment wall and stretched up to look at the top of the tank.

With a half sob of relief Serge saw the still, grotesquely clad form sprawled out. Summoning all his strength, he dragged Chris off the vehicle and struggled to get him inside the tank. Once again the low gravity of the moon was a great help. Under terrestrial conditions he would never have succeeded in lifting the inert form clad in the heavy space suit. As it was, his greatest difficulty was the confined space. At last, sweating profusely, Serge managed to get Chris inside and seal the door.

Feverishly the young Russian examined the helmet on his companion. How did it release? He must remove it before he could get fresh oxygen to the unconscious man; that is, if it wasn't already too late. Almost sobbing in his anxiety, Serge at last discovered how to unfasten the headgear. With fingers that fumbled desperately, he finally freed the helmet and whipped it off the inert young man inside.

Fighting back his natural curiosity to have a close look at his former rival, the Russian began the delicate task of trying to revive him. He decided not to waste valuable time attempting to remove the rest of the space suit. Turning Chris's face downward into a horizontal position on the seat, he began to rock the seat, alternately lowering and raising Chris's head.

Since it was not possible to apply pressure to the chest, because of the space suit, Serge was glad that he knew this other method of artificial respiration. The weight of the stomach organs pressed on the diaphragm and deflated the lungs when the head was low, and the lungs expanded again as the head was raised.

Deliberately Serge enriched the oxygen content of the tank's atmosphere, in spite of using up the valuable supply. Many times during the next hour he despaired of success, but at last he detected the faint action of the patient's muscles. With renewed hope he continued his efforts until gradually Chris's respiration became stronger. The color began to come back into his face, and there was no doubt now that he would be all right!

In another ten minutes the young man on the seat opened his eyes, then struggled upright. He turned and looked at Serge. These two representatives of a divided world, united to combat the perils of this strange satellite, gazed at each other for what seemed a very long time.

CHAPTER 15

Whatever might have happened in the past—it was profitless to dwell on it—Chris and Serge were now inextricably bound together. Neither would have survived without the efforts of the other, and that was all that mattered. Eastern and Western rivalry seemed infantile beyond belief in the face of the challenge of an alien world.

Serge, with an encouraging smile, passed a glucose tube to his companion, who gratefully swallowed some of its contents. During the next few minutes the two young men realized the handicap of not speaking a common language. They managed to learn each other's names, but little else. Then the Russian gave a long report to his ground station. While Chris listened, he wondered whether he would be able to contact Woomera. As soon as Serge finished, he picked up his helmet and spoke into the microphone.

It was no use. Either the casing of the Russian rocket acted as a shield, or he was too far away from Columbus to get his signal across. His radio remained obstinately silent, to his great despair. Seeing his companion's distress, Serge motioned him toward his own radio, obviously inviting Chris to make use of it. But before handing over the mike Serge spoke into it again, asking that someone speaking English might receive a message from the Westerner.

Chris took the microphone and spoke rather shyly into it. He was answered after a brief pause by a voice speaking English with a strong accent. In reply to Chris's request to inform his people that he was safely inside the Russian rocket, Chris was told that it had been arranged for a party of Western scientists to travel to Russia to be present at the landing.

Chris asked the English-speaking Russian to express his sincere thanks to all concerned, then handed the instrument back to Serge. There was a further long and—to Chris—unintelligible exchange. Then he heard the voice speaking English again.

"We have sent on your message as requested," the distant Russian informed him. "You will be told as soon as it is answered. Meanwhile preparations have started for the take-off. You are requested to follow carefully these instructions."

He was told that during the period of acceleration he would have to lie on the floor of the tank and depend upon his space suit to help him withstand the high "g." Smyslov—it was the first time he had heard his companion's surname—would carry out the routine duties in preparation for the take-off. He himself could do little to help, but it would be useful if he kept observation on the conditions outside.

This request puzzled Chris. What was to be gained by maintaining a lookout? What conditions could possibly change in this airless world? Perhaps assigning him this duty was merely a subterfuge to keep him out of the way! But he turned obediently to the television screen which Serge had now connected up to the aerial outside the rocket. The landscape around Lenin was much the same as that around Columbus. The Russian rocket also was in the center of an area blasted clear of dust, and the bare rock was identical to that on which the Western vehicle had landed.

While he was keeping his profitless vigil, Chris was aware that Serge seemed very busy. Between checking masses of instruments, the Russian kept up a continuous report to his control. Many of the fittings inside the tank were strange to Chris. Indeed, the concept of a mobile cabin, which is what the minitank really was, seemed amazing. A thick cable which Serge had connected to a socket in Lenin provided the link between rocket and tank. Truly the Soviets were greatly advanced technically, as their Lunik rockets had proved.

As he performed his duties, Serge frequently flashed a smile of encouragement to the Westerner. Chris longed to be of help to him. He thought wistfully of poor Columbus and reflected that the Russian would have been as useless in the Western projectile as he was here, for the instrumentation of the two rockets was very dissimilar. Rousing himself from these thoughts, Christopher turned again to the glass screen. Then he rubbed his eyes in astonishment.

A thick gray mist had blotted out the distant landscape and was coming nearer the rocket. He called sharply to his companion, and Serge left his work to peer at the screen. He, too, was puzzled at this amazing phenomenon, for with no air or water on this barren world a fog would have seemed impossible. Yet here it was, swirling and twisting as it moved forward menacingly.

Somewhere at the back of his mind Chris remembered reading or being told that mysterious clouds appeared from time to time inside the crater Plato and on several other places on the moon. No explanation could be given for them and not much was known about them. Now it looked as if there was soon going to be an opportunity to experience such a cloud at first hand. A pity there was no means of obtaining a sample!

The Russian returned to his task, after reporting to

control. Christopher continued his observation. There was something a little frightening about the way the mist twisted and eddied about as it moved forward. How could it do this in the absence of air? Watching it closely, Chris saw that the cloud frequently seemed to run together and collect in one spot. Here it became very thick and dense, almost solid looking. Then the knot of vapor would break up and the whole thing would move forward again. For some reason Chris, who had had plenty of experience with London's famous fogs, felt a little frightened at this inexplicable happening. He particularly disliked the concentrations of vapor which seemed, somehow, evil.

Relaxing for a moment, Chris took his eyes from the screen. Heavens above! He was starting to have that peculiar feeling again—the feeling he associated with the space beings who had attacked the Earth. He looked at Serge, wanting to convey a message to him somehow, and he saw that the Russian looked as if he too was very uncomfortable. Again the terrible handicap of language beset them, and they could only gesture to each other. By a sign Chris asked if he could use the microphone, and with a strained nod his companion agreed.

Striving to speak as calmly as he could, Christopher described the advance of the cloud and the sensation he felt. The English-speaking scientist at the other end questioned him closely, but Chris was only able to say that what he was feeling now seemed similar to previous experiences. Even as he spoke he felt the buzzing in his head getting worse.

Toward the end of his report his voice rose a note or two as his composure threatened to leave him. He could see that Serge was no longer carrying out his duties. Instead, he was holding his head with both hands and slowly rocking from side to side. Chris seized him and shook him strongly. The Russian said something unintelligible and shook himself free.

Chris was now in a terrible state. Not only was the feeling in his head getting worse, but he was alarmed because he knew that his companion had become almost useless for the job he was to do. It seemed logical that because of his previous experience he should survive the attack longer than Serge, but how could he help? He was completely lost among the strange array of instruments. Neither could he tell control what jobs had already been completed. Only Serge could ensure their safe take-off—and Serge was now semiconscious.

Desperately Chris slapped the other's face at the same time he shouted to control that the Russian pilot had almost succumbed to the radiation. Control evidently realized the situation quickly. The loudspeaker blared forth a torrent of words in Russian that visibly shook Serge to the core. Feebly he completed one or two operations before he sank to the floor completely unconscious. Chris begged control to get them off this accursed satellite without another second's delay.

It was not going to be that easy, the Russian scientist said, but he promised that Lenin would take off in five minutes. He spoke kindly and encouragingly to Chris, urging him to stay conscious as long as possible, for the fuel pumps must be started just before take-off and he would have to do it. It was on the extreme right of the front panel. If he blacked out before control was ready, then the rocket could not fire and all would be lost. If he could hold out, there was every prospect of a successful launching and a safe journey back to Earth.

Shaking all over, Chris turned away from the loudspeaker, which he had been staring at as if trying to see the face behind that disembodied voice. Five minutes? It was a lifetime. He turned toward the television screen, but it was a complete blank. The cloud had reached the rocket and was pressing all around. Looking out of the rectangular patch of glass screen seemed like looking out a window into a dense fog. Even as he watched, the screen grew darker, as if the rocket itself was enveloped in one of those heavy, frightening concentrations of mist.

The ringing and throbbing in his head were steadily increasing. With an agony of effort Chris struggled to retain consciousness. He remembered a similar fight when he first encountered the space beings. Then he had managed to retain his faculties just long enough to launch the beacon which enabled the atomic rockets to destroy the domes.

Now he had the same grim task again, with the lives of his companion and himself hanging on the result. He remembered how he had got the strength last time to resist for the last few critical seconds. Now, as before, he prayed with all his strength, the sweat rolling down his face.

Would the Russian control never give him the signal? The five minutes seemed like hours—days, even. He couldn't keep his wits much longer. His senses were slipping fast. Was it too late?

"Press the switch in ten seconds from now."

Only ten seconds! But even that seemed too long. Chris swayed and felt he must fall at any minute. Vaguely he heard the Russian begin the count-down, though, oddly, there were gaps in it.

"Nine. Eight. Five. Two. One. NOW."

Even as he realized he must have blacked out during those missing seconds, the buzzing in his head reached a crescendo. Now he was falling and he knew it was the end. His nerveless hand reached out toward the switch. Then all went black.

The jet plane carrying the Western scientists was streaking northward. It was a silent, strained party that sat in the pressurized cabin seven miles above the earth. Sir Leo Frayling stared straight ahead in frigid detachment. Sir George Benson, his face set in deep lines of worry, beat a nervous tattoo on the arm of his seat. Billy Gillanders's mouth was compressed into a

grim, straight line. Wing Commander Greatrex was
hunched up in unaccustomed gloom. In addition to
these four men there were Dr. Rosenberg and the leaders of the other national teams taking part in Operation
Columbus.

To all of them it seemed strange that they were
flying right to the rocket nerve center of their former
rivals. The agreement between East and West to co-
operate was barely a few hours old, and after the long
months of bitter competition it was too new for them
to realize it fully. Frayling hated the secondary role he
would necessarily have to play at the Soviet rocket
base. Benson and the others welcomed the agreement a
little warily, but hoped that it would blossom into
permanent world-wide partnership.

The party had boarded the plane literally at a few
minutes' notice. Once the Communists had agreed to
allow Western scientists into their landing area, no time
was lost—perhaps partly for fear that Russia might
change her mind. Another reason was the desire of
Frayling and his companions to be at the rocket base as
long as possible before Lenin was brought down to
Earth.

Even while the plane was shooting across the Australian continent, messages were coming in from the
Soviet Union about the happenings on the moon. Not
only did this promise well for future East-West relationships, but it also informed Chris's friends of his
perils on Earth's satellite. Every few minutes the radio
officer would bring in to Sir Leo the latest report. The
chief scientist, after reading it silently, would pass it
on to the others.

It was by this means that they learned of the titanic
effort of the two young men to turn over the minitank,
and of Chris's return for the fragment of dome. One
of the worst moments was when the Russians reported
Serge's messages telling of the silence and lack of
signals from the passenger on top of the tank.

Benson guessed that whatever oxygen had been saved by Chris's rest in Columbus had been more than used up in his strenuous efforts to right the minitank. Now he must have completely exhausted his supply. Even as they hurtled along at supersonic speed this young man of whom Benson was so fond must have been making his last few painful gasps.

Wing Commander Greatrex was likewise thinking about his young friend Christopher. It seemed that this time there was nothing he or anyone else could do to help the brave chap who must perish far away from his friends. It was this helplessness that made the usually cheerful officer so depressed.

"The minitank is trying to climb the ramp back into Lenin, but its batteries are almost exhausted."

That was the next message that was passed silently to the group of scientists. Now it seemed that neither of the first two men to land on the moon would return to tell of his experiences. Perhaps, in view of all that had happened, there might be some grim satisfaction if the Russian chap was finished too. But as scientists they would have wished for him to return rather than for both expeditions to fail.

Poor Chris! Sir George recalled vividly the painful episode he'd had with his young friend over volunteering for this project. Now the lad was breathing his last on the satellite he'd longed to visit. The scientist had to stare hard through the plane windows to conceal the smarting of his eyes.

What they expected in the next message from the Russian control, none of the sad little party knew. Surely it could only be to write "The End" to man's first audacious attempt to tread beyond the limits of his own planet. When the radio officer did come in with his slip of paper Sir George continued to stare through the window with unseeing eyes. Would Frayling order the plane to return? he wondered. It seemed useless to go on.

[164]

But what was this? Sir Leo was waving the paper about in a most uncharacteristic way. He positively thrust it at Benson, who forced himself to read it, though scarcely comprehending its contents.

"The minitank has safely entered Lenin. Smyslov has taken your man inside and is attempting artificial respiration."

A cheer went up from the anxious group. At least there was now a chance of the Russian's returning to Earth. Chris—alive or dead—would be on it, not left alone for the rest of time on an empty, friendless world. Whiskers' incurable optimism now reasserted itself. There was more than a chance, he insisted, that Chris would come round and that in a few days' time they would be shaking him by the hand.

Frayling, naturally more cautious, did not think there was much hope. Sir George Benson would not allow himself to think anything. There was no question now of the plane's turning back. It couldn't make the journey fast enough for the men inside. Pray God that the Russian would succeed!

Never had time passed so slowly. A dozen pairs of eyes barely left the door through which the radio officer must come, but it remained obstinately closed. How was that battle for life going up on the moon? Was Chris too far gone to recover? The strain of waiting increased. Even the imperturbable Frayling betrayed his anxiety by the rhythmic tattoo he tapped unconsciously on the arm of his seat. Beads of perspiration glistened on the foreheads of Benson and Greatrex. Still no message from the Russians!

Sir George could stand it no longer. Getting to his feet, he called to Frayling that he was going to ask the radio officer to try and contact the Soviet control for any further news. As Benson turned toward the door it opened, and an excited officer stumbled through.

"He's come around!" he shouted in a most unprofessional manner.

Instantly he was surrounded by the excited members of the party. With difficulty Sir Leo took the paper to read the message aloud.

"Smyslov reports that Godfrey's respirations have started naturally. He is continuing his efforts."

There were tears of relief in more than one pair of eyes at that instant—relief that the young man, whom they had all known and liked, was still alive and might even yet join them once more. The message was passed from hand to hand as it was read and reread. Sir George returned to his seat silently, too full of emotion even to speak.

When word came through that Chris himself had spoken to the Russian control the spirits of the scientists rose intoxicatingly. They began to make silly jokes and wisecracks, at which they laughed uproariously, as the result of the relaxed tension. He'd been right all along, Whiskers proclaimed loudly. He knew Chris would pull through. You couldn't keep a good man down.

When the Soviet scientists informed their Western colleagues that preparations were in hand for Lenin's take-off, all their anxiety seemed over. The next report, describing the lunar mist, aroused great interest, but no disquiet. The scientists speculated among themselves about this mysterious cloud. What a pity, they exclaimed, that neither expedition was equipped to get any information about it. This omission must certainly be remedied on the next flight. The news that Chris and his companion were experiencing the strange radiation associated with the space beings came as a great shock to them all, and anxiety began to creep back.

Their concern was increased sharply when the Russians informed them that Smyslov had succumbed to the radiation, and that Christopher had the task of completing the pretake-off operations. For a second time the party was plunged into gloom—a sharp contrast to its exuberance only a short while before. Again they all felt very helpless and futile, knowing that again there was nothing any living soul could do to help their distant friend.

It seemed that the Soviet scientists were equally apprehensive about the struggle going on a quarter of a million miles away. They explained how important it was that Godfrey should be able to switch on the fuel pumps at the right moment, and that if he too became a victim of the radiation, control would be unable to get the rocket off the moon. Less than five minutes was needed. Could the young Briton hold out?

If Sir George Benson and his colleagues had been depressed when they feared Chris would die from lack of oxygen, their feelings now sank even lower. Perhaps because of the wild swings from fear to joy and back to fear again, they felt even more despondent than before. Every ounce of strength seemed to have been drained from Benson's body. He sat slumped in his seat, not caring whether the plane flew on or crashed.

CHAPTER 16

"Lenin has taken off."

It seemed incredible. Yet such was the message from the Russians. Could there be some error? Could the Soviet scientists be mistaken? Was this some ghastly joke?

No, of course not! Such was the respect of the Western scientists for their Eastern colleagues that the doubt troubled them for no more than a fleeting second. And they knew that the Russians did not play practical jokes. It must be true, then! The rocket had taken off! Chris had resisted the radiation long enough to start the fuel pumps!

Again the atmosphere in the plane became electric with excitement. The dignified scientists danced about and slapped one another's backs. The almost impossible had happened; the million-to-one chance had come off! Even Frayling behaved as few had seen him do before, and tears rolled unashamedly down Sir George's face. Again the plane couldn't fly fast enough for its impatient passengers.

Chris did not know whether or not he had switched on the pumps. He was unconscious as he fell to the cabin floor and sprawled alongside Serge. Neither of them felt the rocket begin to quiver as the fuel was ignited. Neither knew when, within a very few seconds, Lenin tore itself from the evil grasp of the moon mist and began to rise rapidly into the black sky overhead.

Now all the skill of the Russian scientists was called into play, for they must guide the projectile onto its correct flight path back to Earth—a difficult enough task with the help of a pilot, and now, without that assistance, ten times as hard. The delicate maneuver was accomplished at last, and Lenin began its long flight home. Inside the rocket, the two young men remained mercifully unconscious and so escaped the extreme discomfort of the period of acceleration. As they lay there, side by side, the rocket raced on ever farther from the moon and the baleful gray cloud. The mysterious radiation diminished rapidly as the rocket climbed higher and higher.

Lenin had been in free fall for some time when Christopher first showed signs of recovery. Consciousness came back slowly. He felt an excruciating ache in his left leg, which became so painful that it forced him to notice his surroundings.

For a while Chris gazed blankly around. He could not recall at all where he was or what had happened to him. When he straightened out his leg in an effort to ease the cramp, he realized that he was floating about. Even as his memory came flooding back, he felt a bump against him and, turning his head, saw the unconscious Russian floating grotesquely about the mini-tank.

So they had got away! He must have managed that switch, and the chaps back on good old Earth had done the rest. Thank God that terrible buzzing in his head had gone and he was now able to think clearly. His

first job must be to anchor Serge to the seat to prevent
his injuring himself by bumping into the walls. Then
he must speak to the Soviet control and let them know
he was all right.

It wasn't too easy to guide the inert Russian onto
the seat and strap him there. Fortunately Chris had
had considerable experience in working in conditions
of zero gravity, and that helped him accomplish the
task. Chris reached for a glucose tube, for his throat
was so dry that he doubted whether he could manage
even a croak until he had moistened his mouth. That
done, he called into the microphone.

Soon the English-speaking Russian answered. Chris
was able to tell him that Serge and he had survived
the take-off, though Serge was still unconscious. Chris
reported that they were now out of range of the disturbing radiation, and he asked for instructions as to
the duties he could perform. He was told which instruments to read and how to read them, so that the
Soviet control could plot more exactly the path of the
rocket's return.

From time to time Christopher slapped his companion's face in an attempt to bring him back to consciousness. When he did recover, Chris wondered how
they would get on together for two days confined in
such a small space, even though it was larger than his
cabin in poor old Columbus. The thought worried
Chris, for he had heard of the strain that close confinement put on human relationships.

Gradually Serge recovered. After a few preliminary
twitches, he opened his eyes. They stared blankly
ahead, not recognizing his companion or even seeming
to be aware of his presence. With a moan, Serge closed
his eyes again, but reopened them after a few seconds.
This time Chris thought he saw a gleam of intelligence
in them. Then they shut again. Chris slapped the Russian's face gently. The Soviet youth stared for an instant, then looked about the cabin wildly. A torrent of

words poured from his lips but he soon became calmer. He turned to his companion and spoke a word that the Briton had been waiting to hear.

"Chris!" the Russian said with a smile. Chris grinned and called, "Serge!" These words—the only ones they could say to each other—were enough to remind them both of the bond which a common peril had forged between them. Struggling upright, the Russian released his straps, took the microphone, and spoke. There followed a long exchange between Serge and his control which was completely unintelligible to Chris, though twice he heard his own name mentioned. At the end the English-speaking voice came into the cabin.

"Smyslov asks us to give you his thanks," it said a little stiffly. "He now feels fully recovered and able to resume his duties."

"Tell him how glad I am," Chris said with genuine pleasure. "It was just luck that I managed those pumps. Tell him I'll do anything I can to help him, but I don't want to be in his way."

His remarks were translated for the benefit of Serge, who acknowledged them with a smile and a wave. Then he busied himself reading a number of instruments. Chris had an opportunity now to study his companion more closely. So this was the young man who had tried to kill him, or at least prevent his return to Earth, simply because he was a non-Communist!

Since that, however, the Russian had saved his life, just as he had saved the Russian's. So perhaps they were quits. It was strange, though, to be in the company of one whose mental make-up was so different. How would the Russian react to their close confinement for two days? How should they best occupy their time when Serge was not busy with his duties?

Serge had been having similar thoughts. He was to be in contact with this young Western imperialist for a considerable period. Would Chris adopt a superior attitude, even though he was making the flight home in a Russian rocket, with a Russian pilot, and using the Russian guidance system? And what could they do when his duties were over?

If we could speak to each other, Chris said to himself, there'd be such a lot to talk about!

We will learn each other's language. Then I can convert him to Communism, Serge decided silently.

Each for his own reason, the two young men began the laborious process of trying to understand one another. It was doubly difficult without books or the help of someone knowing both languages. Still, they persevered. With the aid of drawings, each gradually built up a vocabulary of some hundred words. They first learned the name in both languages of everything inside the minitank. Then they began very simple sentences. It was a long and often irritating process, and both Serge and Chris often found themselves out of patience with the other.

"Why is he so slow to understand?" each one thought. At the end of one particularly exasperating period they turned from each other in disgust.

Periodically Serge would transmit instrument readings to his control. Occasionally the English-speaking scientist would talk to Chris, but the whole journey was becoming increasingly monotonous. One moment of terrific excitement, however, came for Chris when quite unexpectedly a new voice sounded over the radio. It was speaking English, and, incredibly, it was the voice of Sir George Benson!

The British scientist explained that their plane had landed for refueling and that the Russians had thought to arrange this delightful radio hook-up. To Chris, it was wonderful to hear the voice of his friend again. To Benson, it was nothing short of miraculous that he could again talk with the young man whom he had given up as lost. The two friends talked together excitedly until someone at the Russian control interrupted politely but firmly, so that Serge could make another series of reports on their position.

Perhaps it was reaction after the excitement of the unexpected contact with Sir George that gave Chris his first feeling of positive dislike for his fellow passenger. What was the use of trying to understand his language? They were miles apart in background and outlook, and always would be. How many more hours would this hateful journey last? Perhaps he could sleep some of the time away.

Serge looked at his companion with growing disgust. What a relief it would be to get back to Earth! He was sure now that he could detect a cynical sneer on the capitalist's face. What did he have to be so superior about, anyway? And to think that he had befriended the emissary of the imperialists! If only his minitank had not met with that wretched misfortune, he would not have been saddled with this disdainful fellow passenger. Well, in another twenty-four hours, if all went well, he'd be rid of him forever.

Hours passed as the two young men stared at each other in glum silence. They had fastened themselves to opposite sides of the tank, for in the confined space which they occupied a collision was only too easy, and nothing could be more irritating or provocative for each than to have the other fellow floating forcibly into him. Chris dozed fitfully, but Serge felt little desire for sleep. All he wanted was to see the last of that detested face opposite.

Lenin had been under the influence of Earth's gravity for many hours, and was now falling freely toward it at an increasing speed. The landing would be a delicate operation, requiring the utmost co-operation between control and the pilot inside. Serge could have been thinking about the job he would have to do in a few hours' time, instead of occupying his thoughts exclusively with his increasing animosity toward the Westerner.

[174]

As Chris slept, the Russian looked at him intently. Even the way his companion breathed was hateful now to Smyslov, and it took a considerable effort to restrain himself from smacking a fist into that face.

Not knowing how close he'd been to open hostility, Chris soon roused from his uneasy doze. Heavens, how that chap Smyslov was staring at him! Hadn't he anything better to do? Perhaps, Chris thought, he'd better not sleep again. There was no knowing what the Communist might do. After all, he'd made one attempt at his life! Yes, he'd better watch Serge pretty closely from now on.

So the two young men glared at each other warily. In Chris, Serge saw the personification of all the imperialists he'd ever heard about, with their arrogant trampling on the rights of others for their own profit. Here was a symbol of all he had been taught to hate and despise; all that the Communists were fighting against; all that threatened danger to the Soviet State. On his side, Chris regarded Serge as the product of a system of ruthless State tyranny, where the individual was not allowed to think or criticize and where opponents were quietly exterminated.

Neither of the two rocket travelers knew that they were the first victims of a strange effect on the mind caused by a long period of weightlessness when in intimate contact with an unsuitable companion. On the outward journey each had been alone, Chris under an anesthetic. Now that they were together a temperamental explosion was building up. Would they tolerate each other until Lenin returned to Earth, or would something spark off the clash between them?

At about this time the Western jet plane was landing at the airfield attached to the Soviet rocket base. As Sir Leo Frayling led his party down the landing steps, Professor Boronoff stepped forward to shake their hands cordially. It was a great relief to the Russian scientist once again to be working with, instead of against, his old colleagues. Greetings over, he gave them the latest position of Lenin. Something about the professor gave Sir George the impression that he was a worried man. He was right. As soon as Boronoff had inquired the rocket's latest position he called Frayling and Benson to one side.

"All is not well aboard Lenin," he confided. "I am worried about our two young men. Smyslov is not performing his duties well. There seems to be some tension. Oh, we have nothing definite to go on, but it is surprising how little sounds coming over the radio build up an impression of 'atmosphere.' You know—a snort, an intake of breath, a muttered exclamation, even a silence. They have stopped trying to learn each other's language, and there is no attempt at conversation. If there is trouble between them it can be serious. The landing operation requires the utmost concentration. It will not be possible if our two young men work against each other."

"I see," Frayling said slowly. "But I'm sure we can get our man to see sense. I will speak to him."

"It's not as easy as that, Sir Leo," the Russian explained. "We have done everything to control Smyslov, but he has not responded. I fear you will have the same difficulty with Godfrey."

"Perhaps I might manage it," Benson said quietly. They went into the radio room and he took the microphone. For ten minutes he spoke, trying to cajole a word from Chris, but it was useless. In the speeding rocket Chris and Serge were oblivious to everything except a burning hatred for each other. Nothing that came over the loudspeaker meant a thing to them. Whether Russian or English was spoken, neither knew nor cared. All that each was aware of was the burning eyes of the other.

The Russian allowed Sir George to try again and again, but it was useless. Anxiously the scientist listened to catch the slightest sound. His colleagues watched him, trying to gain a clue about the situation in the rocket. Suddenly all color drained from Benson's face. He took off the earphones and placed them down.

"They're fighting," he said tersely.

CHAPTER 17

Chris had no idea what started it. One moment he and Serge were glaring at each other. The next second they were locked in combat. Round and round the minitank they floated like performers in a fantastic flying ballet. Never before had there been such a strange fight. Never before had punches had such an amazing result. As each blow landed, the combatants flew apart to crash into the sides of the tank. Both were soon bleeding freely, as much from the broken instruments as from each other's fists.

Completely regardless of the torrent of words that poured from the loudspeaker in both Russian and English, the two young men fought on. Fists and feet flew in a mad whirl. Bodies crashed, heads bumped, faces were flattened as they collided with parts of the tank and with each other. In silent fury the combat continued while Lenin streaked ever nearer to Earth. Soon it would be entering the outer fringes of the atmosphere. Then the landing maneuver should be started if the projectile were not to crash as an incandescent ball of fire on some distant part of the globe.

The control scientists of all nations gathered in the

Soviet control looked at one another helplessly. Pleas, threats, appeals had all failed to stop the struggle going on in the heavens. Now try as they might, the men on Earth could not get the rocket to respond to their impulses, for many of the vital pieces of apparatus had been damaged in that insane duel. Having carefully provided against all foreseeable accidents, the rocket builders had left out of their calculations the greatest of all hazards—the human element.

Blindly the two combatants swam about the small compartment, heedless of the damage their struggle was causing. Dials, gauges, switches were smashed and bent by the impact of their bodies. One switch had so far escaped. It was that which would ignite the retro-rocket in the event the impulse from control failed to function. Now—call it chance or divine Providence, as you will—the tangled bodies fell against the switch at just the moment control would have chosen. Unintentional though it was, the circuit was completed, and the retro-rocket roared into life.

In the next instant the battle was over as Chris and Serge were flattened against the tank floor by the terrific deceleration. Quite unprepared for the ordeal, they found the strain intolerable. No longer were they at each other's throats. They could think only of the torture, this unbearable pressure that seemed to be crushing them. Unconsciousness came quickly to them both.

"The retro-rocket has been fired," one of the Russian scientists shouted. At once the control room was in a turmoil. All those present had resigned themselves to the destruction of the rocket and its passengers. Now, at the eleventh hour, a most important thing had happened. Lenin was being slowed down more or less as it had been planned. Had one of the two young men had the sense to press the switch? Or had the motor been ignited by some lucky accident?

There was no way of finding out. Over the radio there was only silence.

"They must have passed out," Benson muttered, and that seemed to be the general opinion. It was certain that the unhappy conflict was over, but what was to happen now? Unless the retro-rocket could be accurately controlled, which could now be done only by one of Lenin's passengers, the projectile would shoot off again into space, never to return. Both Western and Eastern scientists could only listen and wait.

The red mist in front of Christopher's eyes seemed to be getting lighter. He groaned as he tried to raise his head, then let it sink back to the floor from the sheer agony of the effort. Slowly his wits came back as he lay there, pinned down by the terrific deceleration. He struggled to recall what had happened.

One very strong impression that forced itself into his mind was that he and Serge had had some sort of fight. Try as he would, he could not get rid of this uncomfortable thought. It became strong enough to prompt him to try and raise his head again. This time, by using all his returning strength, he managed to lift it a few inches and even turn it to one side before letting it fall back.

That brief look was enough. Serge lay near him, still unconscious, and showing all the signs of a fierce struggle. Now he came to think of it, Chris could feel the soreness of his own face and body, and there was an unmistakable taste of blood from cut and swollen lips. So they had been fighting! What on earth had made them do that?

Turning his head again he could see unmistakable signs of struggle all around the compartment. It must have been pretty fierce, judging from the broken instruments! Why had they done it? he kept asking himself. What had started it all?

Now that he was conscious again he must let control know. He tried to call out, but his muscles were still immobilized by the pressure and he could manage only a strangled cry. It was enough! A voice on the loudspeaker spoke urgently but in Russian, and he did not understand. (A pity he had not gained more knowledge of the language from Serge.) Then came the voice of Sir George, strained and anxious.

"Chris, are you conscious? Are you all right, Chris? Can you turn down the fuel valve? You must turn down the fuel valve. Can you hear?"

Chris managed a sound intended to convey that he heard. So he was to reduce the fuel supply. Easier said than done. Fortunately he knew which was the fuel valve; the difficulty would be getting to it and turning it. If only this pressure would ease a little! But it would not do that until the thrust of the motor had been reduced; that is, until the valve had been turned. Well, he'd have to attempt it. Uncle George had sounded pretty worried, so it must be very important. Couldn't those chaps in control turn off the juice? Apparently not; otherwise they wouldn't be so worked up about it.

Exerting all his strength, Chris inched himself toward the valve. Fortunately Serge was not in the way; otherwise it would have been impossible for Chris to climb over his body or to move it.

Ah, he was nearly there! Another inch, and another. Now if only he could raise his hand a few inches he could reach the valve. Doggedly he tried, but his arm seemed heavier than lead. His face was distorted by the pressure and the agony of his effort. Up, up went his hand, fingers groping for the wheel. For a second they touched it, then slid off. Now again. That was better. His fingers curled around the wheel and he was able to hold them there. Could he turn it? A few degrees would be sufficient. Could he?

Ah-h-h, it had moved! Chris managed to give it about a quarter turn before sinking back to the floor exhausted. As he lay there laboring for breath he felt sure the terrific thrust of the retro-rocket had been reduced. He would try to raise his hand again. It was easier this time, and he gave the wheel of the valve a full turn.

Within seconds Chris could feel the thrust die away. It was still considerable, but he was now able to sit up and look around. Serge seemed in bad shape, and the tank was a shambles. Surely they couldn't have caused all that damage? What had it all been about, anyway?

"Fuel valve partly closed," he was now able to call out.

"Yes, we can see you've managed it," Benson's voice came back full of relief. "Only just in time. What's been happening up there?"

Chris felt himself flush with shame.

"I—I don't quite know," he stammered. "I think we've been scrapping."

"I should jolly well think you have," Sir George called back. "Do you know you've smashed everything up and we can't do a thing from here?"

"Yes, it looks like it," the young man answered ruefully. "I'm afraid I'm very hazy about it."

"How's the other chap?"

"He's still out. No, wait a bit. I think he's coming round. Yes, he's opened his eyes."

"Let him come on the radio as soon as he can. I gather it's going to be a tricky job bringing Lenin down," the scientist concluded.

Chris turned from the microphone and knelt by the Russian. Raising his head with one hand, with the other he placed the end of a glucose tube in Serge's mouth and squeezed. Soon Serge was sitting up and looking round.

"Thank you, Chris," he said. So he hadn't forgotten the little English he'd been taught! Sometimes in Russian, more often in English, but most of all by gestures, the Westerner tried to tell his companion what had happened. Serge, too, it seemed, was at a complete loss to know why they had fought. The whole episode now seemed like a ghastly nightmare.

"Your control wants you, if you can get to the mike," Chris said, pointing. Serge struggled to his feet and made for the instrument. Then there was a long exchange between the Russian and control, very little of which Godfrey could follow. Well, at least for some reason they weren't ticking Serge off as he'd expected they would. Instead, he gathered they were giving him a string of instructions for the landing.

When the flow of Russian had finished, Benson's voice sounded again.

"Hello, Chris," it called. "We think your scrap was somehow caused by your being in free fall, but we'll find out for sure later. The Russian chap can't explain it any more than you. Now you're under gravity it won't happen again. The local team is handling the re-entry, of course, but we'll be on hand when you touch down. Good luck."

"Thanks. I'll be seeing you," Godfrey called back hopefully. He was fully conscious of the danger of landing without direct help of control. Would Serge be able to bring it off? He felt helpless as he watched his companion do all the work.

The altimeter had been put out of action, so information about Lenin's height above the Earth had to come from observations taken by ground stations. Chris could hear control calling out the distance with monotonous regularity. He had learned enough from Serge to be able to translate most of the reports.

"One hundred and sixty-three miles. One hundred and fifty-eight."

Down in the Soviet headquarters the scientists of many nations anxiously watched a large chart on one of the walls. On it the desired landing maneuver had been carefully worked out in terms of the rocket's velocity at different heights. This was indicated by a strong red line on the graph. The idea was to keep Lenin's altitude and speed, when plotted on the graph, as near to the red line as possible by ordering the fuel valve to be opened or closed to vary the rate of fall. It was a nerve-wracking business for Boronoff and his colleagues on Earth, and for the two young men in the approaching projectile.

A further complication was caused by the need to make the landing as near to the control station as possible. Small rockets at the side of the main one thrust the vehicle in the required direction. Nevertheless all the men in that densely packed room breathed a sigh of relief when the Russian professor announced that Lenin was now following the red line.

There was, too, a grin of relief on Serge's face as he turned to Chris with the news. It seemed that except for some dire accident the landing would now be a success and that they would soon be meeting their friends.

CHAPTER 18

Unknown to Chris and Serge, and to their friends on Earth, disaster was rushing toward Lenin at a speed of twenty thousand miles an hour. All of them had recognized the danger of the space vehicle's being struck by a meteor, though it was known to be very remote. Earth, Chris knew, was constantly being bombarded with fast-moving bits of matter from somewhere out in space, most of them no larger than a grain of sand. These particles, known as meteorites, were, he knew, burned up by the atmosphere before they reached the ground.

He was aware that satellites and high-altitude rockets had recorded this perpetual shower, but never had one encountered a particle of any size. It had always been reckoned that a space vehicle being struck by a meteor the size of a marble was something which could happen only once in several thousand years. By the most cruel luck such a meteor was streaking toward Lenin at that very moment.

As Serge bent to open the fuel valve, there was a blinding flash across the minitank like a bolt of lightning. It happened so quickly that the two young men were frozen into immobility with surprise, rather than fear. The flash seemed to have gone from one side of the compartment to the opposite side, right between them. Where it had touched the metal there was a glow of heat, and in the center of each glow was a round hole about an inch in diameter.

Instantly they both realized what had happened. A small meteor had passed right through Lenin!

The next second both Chris and Serge jumped into action. It was of vital importance that the holes should be sealed, so that the precious oxygen would not be sucked out by the vacuum of space. What could they use to stop up the holes? There seemed to be nothing in the tank for such an emergency. In poor old Columbus, Chris remembered, there had been things like bicycle patches that one could stick over any small hole in the casing.

Frantically Chris and Serge looked around the wreckage-littered tank. Already the pressure of their atmosphere was falling and their breathing was becoming labored. In a short time all the air in the compartment would be drawn out and their lungs would burst in the vacuum left behind. The Russian tore off a strip of clothing and rammed it into the hole nearest him. It was immediately sucked through into the void beyond. There was nothing, nothing, with which to seal those deadly holes!

Then Chris had an inspiration. From somewhere in the back of his mind came the memory of a story he'd heard as a child of the Dutch boy who had plugged a hole in a dyke with his arm, stopping the inflow of water until help came. Now the problem was not to stop water from pouring in but air from gushing out. But perhaps the same device would serve. It was worth trying, anyway.

Reaching forward, Christopher put his palm over the hole. Then he yelled out in agony. The hot metal scorched his flesh, but he held it there. From the pressure on his hand he knew that the air was no longer getting out. He—he could stick the pain if it was doing the job.

"Look, Serge," he called, the pain causing perspiration to roll down his face. "I've stopped this one."

The Russian did not fully understand his friend's words, but what he had done was plain. It was also plain to see the agony he was in, and why. Serge did not hesitate. Over the other hole went his hand. His senses reeled with the pain. But the two holes were sealed, and the oxygen was no longer escaping.

"Can—can you still reach—the valve?" Chris gasped. It was essential that the instructions from control should still be followed. With an effort Serge stretched out his free hand. He could just touch the wheel.

"Good!" Godfrey called encouragingly. "Now let control know we're ready to carry on."

It was more a crash than a touchdown. Lenin lay on the Earth amid a cloud of smoke and steam. Its long and perilous journey was over; it lay twisted and broken on a rough, stony plain. Within minutes a huge Soviet helicopter had landed alongside the damaged rocket and a score of men poured out to render what aid they could to the two young men inside. Boronoff, Frayling, Benson and the rest followed in another machine. Nationality, political beliefs, recent history, all were forgotten in the scientists' desperate anxiety to rescue the first two humans to have landed on the moon.

How had Serge and Chris fared? The meteor which had struck them had left a trail plainly visible on the radar screens. That they had survived the impact was inexplicable, yet someone aboard must still be alive, for the landing maneuver had been completed. But what shape were they in? Would they be able to tell of their journey to and from Earth's satellite?

By the time the scientists had landed, the Russian in charge of the ground crew had completed his examination.

"We have heard no sound from inside," the man reported to Boronoff. "The hatch fastenings are twisted and will require cutting. We have located the holes where the meteor entered and left the rocket. It must have passed through the minitank inside."

Benson and his Western colleagues noted the machine-like efficiency of the Russian crew working to open the rocket. There was nothing the Western scientists could do but pace about waiting for the entrance to be made. Sir George should by now have been used to his young friend's repeated peril of death. Many times he had been racked with anxiety, followed by tremendous relief, only to be succeeded by anxiety again. This time it would be all over one way or another. Would Christopher have survived this last peril? If so, would his thirst for adventure now be satisfied?

At a shout from one of the workmen, everyone ran to the hatch. The men had succeeded in opening it. The tank inside could be seen and there was still the problem of getting into it. Boronoff shouted instructions to the crew. One of the men squeezed inside, between the minitank and the rocket casing, and disconnected the little vehicle. The helicopter rose and hovered above. A steel cable was lowered from it and was secured to the tank. At a signal from the crew leader the helicopter slowly rose, lifting the minitank clear of its parent rocket. Gently it deposited the tank on the rocky ground.

As the men raced to unfasten the tank they could clearly see the two sinister holes in its sides. Benson felt his throat contract. Frayling's face was pale. Wing Commander Greatrex was unnaturally silent. Only Professor Boronoff seemed unaffected, but this was because his was the responsibility of directing the operation. He stood close to the minitank while the other scientists waited in a silent semicircle a dozen yards away. All eyes were on the mechanics who were struggling to open the entrance to the little vehicle.

Everyone unconsciously stepped forward as at last the door swung open. Boronoff was the first to clamber up and peer into the dark interior, then disappear inside. Time stood still. The professor's stay inside the tank seemed hours to all; to Sir George Benson it seemed an eternity.

As Boronoff's head reappeared the semicircle broke and scientists and mechanics waited breathlessly for his report. His face was pale and set as he spoke, first in Russian and then in English.

"They are both alive," he said, "but unconscious. Each has a hand which is badly burned. These two young men have again saved each other—and our expedition—by sealing the meteor holes with their palms."

A team of medical men took Chris and Serge into their care.

Several weeks later the two young men were propped up in beds alongside each other in a spotless Russian hospital ward. Serge's left hand was heavily bandaged; Chris's right. They were cheerful and excited, as they looked forward to an official visit. By now each could speak the other's language quite well. Serge insisted on speaking in English, and Christopher in Russian.

Boronoff, Frayling, Benson, Rosenberg and several other leaders came in and stood around the two beds. The atmosphere was lighthearted, almost gay. After the preliminary conversation Chris posed the question both Serge and he had been waiting to ask.

"What have you made of it all?" he demanded eagerly.

"You brought back a tremendous amount of scientific information," Sir George Benson said, speaking for all of them. "The dome fragment has us puzzled, but we're still working on it. The recordings of the reports from each of you will be carefully studied. And I am glad to tell you that this is to be done together, by East and West. We know now that we can make the most progress by co-operating."

The two young men looked at each other and smiled. Their two good hands stretched out and clasped in a tight and friendly grip.